Also by Ian Caro

-

The Overlooked

SPURN

IAN CARO

IJH Books

First published in 2023 by IJH Books, Cowes, Isle of Wight

ISBN 978-1-9161117-3-8

Text copyright © Ian Caro

Cover image and jacket design © IJH Books

Printed on the Isle of Wight by Raven Print & Design

A CIP catalogue for this book is available from the British Library

to

sea anemone

For never was a story of more woe
Than this of Juliet and her Romeo

William Shakespeare, *Romeo and Juliet*

Part One

1

'Now then. What's this?'

'A contract.'

'I can see it's a contract, Jonty. It says "Contract" at the top.'

'Well, then,' says Jonty.

Jonty sits.

He slides the contract across the desk towards Oliver.

Oliver says, 'Were you born in a barn?'

'No need for the door,' says Jonty. 'This won't take long.'

'What are you showing it to me for?'

'Approval.'

Oliver slides the contract back across the desk. He says, 'Isn't that what we pay you for? To approve these things?'

'It's unusual.' Jonty slides it half way back. 'It's not an ordinary contract.'

He sits back, folds his arms and looks Oliver in the eye.

Beyond the diamond-leaded windows, winter continues.

Oliver says, 'Is it chilly in here?'

Jonty shrugs. '-ish. Maybe.'

'Chilly-ish? You should have said.' Oliver gestures towards the ancient cast-iron radiator. 'Shall I - ?'

'No need,' says Jonty. 'It won't take long.' What he means is, It'll take as long as it takes.

Oliver sighs. He glances at the cover sheet. 'What's unusual about it?'

'It's a location contract.' There's a note of pride in Jonty's voice. 'For a film.'

'A film?'

'A Hollywood film.' Jonty mimes a movie camera. 'Romeo and Juliet.'

'The Earl's not going to like that. Luvvies trampling all over the estate.'

'It's not the Earl's decision,' says Jonty. 'Not any more. The Trustees call the shots now.'

'He is a Trustee.'

'But he can't act alone,' says Jonty. 'It's a majority decision. Two signatures will suffice.'

He leans back in his chair. He repeats, 'The Trustees call the shots now.'

In fact it's Jonty who calls the shots now. His influence is everywhere, spreading like the ivy that eats away at the historic walls of the family seat and winds itself round the ancient trees in the spinney, slowly strangling them in the process. They all see it but none of them notice.

'He's still the Earl,' says Oliver.

'You're still the heir.'

4

And the most persuadable Trustee, thinks Oliver. Three Trustees, two signatures. Always Jonty and whoever Jonty persuades. The "Persuader" and the "Persuadee," Jonty would call them. Jonty would draw the inverted commas in the air.

Jonty waits. He knows how to wield silence.

Oliver says, 'He won't like it.'

I don't like it, is what Oliver means. He wants peace and quiet. He wants solitude. He's the thirteenth Earl-in-waiting but he wants to be ordinary. In fact, he thinks, '-in-waiting' is wrong. 'in-waiting' suggests eagerness, anticipation, when what he feels is resignation. Not the thirteenth Earl-in-waiting but the thirteenth Earl-to-be. Come what may.

Jonty says, 'Think of it as a necessary evil.'

Oliver knows Jonty means the contract - the disruption a film unit will bring to the Mundayne family seat - but he could just as well be talking about the title. Earl of Eoferwic. Who wants to be Earl of somewhere no one can pronounce? Oliver has heard all the variations. Yoffer-wyke, Everwick, Effer-wik.

Eff-off-erwic.

Jonty interrupts Oliver's reverie. He says, 'What's Jonty's First Law of Contracts?'

Oliver sighs again. 'There's only one clause that counts.'

'Exactly.'

Jonty pushes the contract towards Oliver, turns over the cover sheet and stabs his forefinger at clause three, pinning the contract to the desk.

'One clause,' says Jonty. 'The consideration. The price of the promise, it's called. The money clause. And that,' he says, tapping his finger on the money clause, 'is a lot of money.'

Oliver says, 'My mind misgives. No good will come of it.'

'You what?'

'Shakespeare,' says Oliver. 'Romeo and Juliet.'

'I don't know anything about Romeo and Juliet.'

'We did it for GCSE.'

'GCSE?' says Jonty. 'Don't remember anything about that. I winged mine.'

'Of course.'

'I had more important things to think about.'

'As ever.'

'The only thing exams examine,' says Jonty, 'is how good you are at exams. Jonty's First Law of Exams - tell them what they want to hear. Jonty's First Law of Everything, actually. Tell them what they want to hear.'

'Romeo doesn't want to get involved,' says Oliver. He slides the contract back across the desk towards Jonty. 'He knows it will end in tears. From the very start he knows it will all go horribly wrong. But his right hand man pushes him into it.'

'Nothing will go wrong,' says Jonty, sliding the contract back. 'Trust me, I'm a lawyer.'

Oliver repeats, 'No good will come of it.'

'Orvane is crumbling,' says Jonty. He raises his palms to indicate the chilly wood-panelled room they sit in. He waits, letting his gesture ripple outwards until it encompasses the rest of the Hall, then the outbuildings, then the lawns and the meadows and the fountains and the ha-ha and the pasture, all of which, they both know, are slowly falling into decay. When Jonty feels his gesture has expanded via strangled spinney and heathered moorland to the very boundaries of the Earldom he resumes. 'This,' he says, tapping his finger again on the money clause, 'will keep it going.'

'What happened to not accepting the first offer?' asks Oliver. 'First Law of Negotiation, you said.'

'This isn't the first offer,' says Jonty. He's pleased with himself. 'It's the third. And Jonty's Second Law of Negotiation is to accept the Third Offer.'

'So you've already done the deal?'

'I've haggled. That's what you pay me for, to haggle, and I'm very good at it. I forced them into making a third offer but the sealing of the deal requires approval. It requires the signatures of at least two Trustees. You and I will suffice.' Jonty smiles. He knows how to use his looks to put the less well blessed at a disadvantage. With a flourish he conjures a gleaming Mont Blanc from the inside pocket of his jacket. Still smiling, head at a slight angle, he uncaps the plush pen and proffers it between forefinger and thumb.

The nib gleams in the wintry light.

Oliver looks at the pen. It's the wrong shape, he thinks. Too round, or too short. Or both. Like me. Yet somehow it looks sure of itself. It looks solid, dependable. It looks as if it knows its place in the world. It looks self assured.

Jonty waits, pen still proffered. He raises an eyebrow, waggles the pen.

Oliver doesn't take it. Instead he asks, 'Is that a trick you learned in law school?'

Jonty tries a different tack. He recaps the Mont Blanc, places it carefully on the desk, sits back, steeples his fingertips. He says, 'It's our duty as Trustees to consider the benefits to the Trust. Apart from the' – he clears his

7

throat – '*funds* there's the PR. Imagine it. Orvane Hall on the silver screen. Izzie Markham waxing lyrical on the West Balcony.' He stands, puts his right hand on his heart, extends his left, gazes at the winter sky beyond the diamond-leaded window and declaims, 'Romeo, Romeo, where are you, Romeo?'

'Wherefore,' says Oliver.

'Exactly,' says Jonty. He sits, re-steeples his fingers and returns his gaze to Oliver. 'Her fans will come flocking to see where it happened. To stand where she stood. To feel what she felt as she uttered those immortal words. That's the bit people remember - Juliet's desperation to know where Romeo is. They'll come flocking.'

'Who is Izzie Markham?'

'A star.'

'No good will come of it,' Oliver says again.

'Imagine the merchandise,' says Jonty. 'The mugs, the T-shirts. The key rings. We'll need to recruit extra staff to help Amanda in the gift shop.'

'Mandy Howe needs no help,' says Oliver. 'The Howes have run that gift shop for generations. Mandy is part of the furniture.'

'Think of the marketing opportunities. We can do star-cross'd weddings.'

'Star-cross'd is a bad thing,' says Oliver. 'They die at the end. There's a pact.'

'This contract,' says Jonty, 'will secure the future.'

'Whose future? Lizzie Markham's?'

'Izzie,' says Jonty. 'No. Her future is already secure. Orvane's.'

'I'll think on it,' says Oliver.

8

They both know Oliver will capitulate. They both know 'thinking on it' is code for delaying the inevitable. Oliver sighs. He knows the Trust can't afford to turn down the money. Perhaps Jonty is right.

But Jonty, over-confident, misjudges his next move. 'Mark my words,' he says, 'Izzie Markham will put Orvane on the map.'

Oliver bangs his fist on the table. 'Orvane is already on the map, Jonty. Orvane has been on the map for nine hundred years. Orvane has been on the map since the Normans pushed their way north. My ancestors created this land. They drew the bloody map.'

Jonty says nothing. This time the silence belongs to Oliver.

'Talking of maps,' says Oliver, 'why the hummer are they doing Romeo and Juliet in the East Riding? It's supposed to be in Italy.'

Jonty remains silent.

'Don't tell me there's a question you can't answer, Jonty. Why the East Riding?'

'I don't know,' says Jonty. 'Because Shakespeare was a Yorkshireman?'

'Shakespeare a Yorkshireman! You great blatherskite. Shakespeare was like you, Jonty – a bloody southerner.'

2

Beyond the high windows of a gleaming Los Angeles skyscraper the deep blue air is endless.

Staring deeply into the endless blue, his back to the reflective surfaces of the thirty-third floor climate-controlled conference room, stands David Campanile. The deep blue of his perfectly cut wrinkle-resistant slim-fit suit matches the deep blue of the sky. The polished toes of his patent-leather shoes stand a hair's breadth shy of the floor-to-ceiling window. Each reflects the other: the polished toes and the high windows.

Far below the polished toes, the city of angels shimmers in the smog-stained heat haze.

Campanile presses his fingers against the cool, sun-comprehending glass - the membrane that separates him from the abyss - and looks upwards, into the blue. A distant glint of fuselage reinforces his wish to be elsewhere. 'Thinking about it?' he says, with his fingers to the glass and his back to the room. 'What is there to think about, Anna?'

Anna addresses the back of the blue suit. 'They didn't give a reason. Their attorney just said they were thinking about it.'

Campanile doesn't respond.

Anna adds, 'Actually, he said thinking *on* it.'

'What does that mean?'

'It means thinking about it.'

Skyscraper, thinks Campanile. Curious term. Naive. Left over from an age of wonder. It belongs in an encyclopaedia of obsolete concepts. Now, they're just towers. Now, it's an everyday occurrence, scraping the sky. You press the button for the elevator and engineering does the rest. He turns away from the window and his polished toes and his blue suit turn with him. He's lean. Some would say lithe. He looks at Anna. 'You told me the deal was done.'

'Their attorney said the deal was done. He said the signatures were a formality. Two signatures, he said. Him and one other Trustee. Now he says they're thinking about it.'

'I don't like rejection,' says Campanile. 'I want to know why. I need a reason.'

'It's not a rejection, David. They're thinking about it.'

'Same thing.'

Anna waits. She knows there's more.

Campanile says, 'Is this a tactic?'

'This is not a tactic, David. They don't know how to haggle. This guy Fullerton-Bagshawe thinks he's greased me up with Vaseline and screwed me backwards over a barrel. Jonty. Ridiculous name. Couldn't hide his delight when he thought he'd forced me into making a third offer. Jonty Fullerton-Bagshawe couldn't haggle his way out of a grocer's bag.'

11

'If it's not the money what is it?' snaps Campanile. 'What happened to the special relationship? I extended the hand of friendship across the ocean and they're throwing it back in my face.'

'They're throwing your hand back in your face?'

'You know what I mean, Anna. I extended my hand and now I'm on the back foot.'

Anna waits.

'I don't like being on the back foot, Anna. We need to regain control of the situation. We need to be in the driver's seat.' He paces the length of the conference table. He reaches a decision. 'Offer them more money.'

'More money?'

'Show them where the power lies.'

'More money sends the wrong message, David.'

'OK, tell them to take a hike. Tell them we don't want their location. Tell them it's their loss. Sal, how badly do we want this location? Why do we want this location? Why the hell are we setting Romeo and Juliet in England, anyway? It's supposed to be in Italy.'

'For Christ's sake!' Sal bangs his fist on the conference table. 'I've told you before, David. I've told you countless times. My movie is not set in England. It will be filmed in England but the setting is... elsewhere. The setting is mystical. It's fantastical. The setting is' - Sal makes an expansive double-handed European gesture - 'everywhere and nowhere.'

'Your movie?' says Campanile. '*Your* movie? Who's paying for the damn thing? This picture is a Belltower Production. It belongs to Belltower Studios.'

'Your precious studios won't have a movie without a director.'

'I can always find another director, Sal.'

12

'Every movie you say you will find another director, David. Every movie. But you never do. You will never find another Masuccio Salernitano. There is only one Masuccio Salernitano.'

'Children, please,' says Anna.

'Actually,' says Sal, 'there are two. The other was a poet. He wrote J- '

Campanile cuts him off. 'How badly do we want this location?'

'Very,' says Sal.

'Why? If the setting is so fantastical why can't we create it here, in the back lot? Or CGI it?'

'David, David,' says Sal. 'This is why you are the producer and I am the director. You have no imagination. No flair. No vision. Only at Orvane can my vision be realised. Only at Orvane. Orvane is... Avalon.'

'But *why*, Sal?' says Campanile. 'I need to know *why*.'

'Why so linear, David? Always so *linear*.'

'I need to know why. Give me a reason I can hold on to. Something I can touch.'

'There's a castle,' says Sal. 'There's a balcony. There's a church. The perfect church. And a town with an unpronounceable name. Unpronounceable! Like an incantation. The Earl owns the town. It's named after him. Or the other way round.'

'How do you know all this?' asks Campanile.

'How does anyone know anything?'

'How?'

'Recce,' says Sal.

'Recce,' echoes Campanile. He ponders the military connotations, as he does every time anyone uses the term. Reconnoitre. Perhaps it's apt. Making movies is like a

13

military operation, after all. The logistics. He says, 'You went to England on a recce? When? Who paid?'

'Jonty showed me round,' says Sal. 'Charming man. Charming! And you paid, David. It's your movie, remember. You paid for my flights and you paid for Jonty's pheasant biriyani. A Yorkshire delicacy, according to Jonty. Local pheasant, chefs from Bradford. Jonty paired it with Black Sheep and you paid for that, too. His biriyani had lead shot in it. '

'Who authorised a recce? Anna, did you authorise a recce?'

Sal says, 'It's perfect, David. Everything is there, in one location. On one estate. It's magical. All the ley lines in England pass through it. And Mantua itself is nearby.'

'Mantua?'

'Read the screenplay, David. You never read the God-damned screenplay. Mantua. Where Romeo is exiled for killing Tybalt. Mantua is crucial. Crucial! It's where it all goes wrong. It's where wires get crossed. Where communication breaks down. It's the crux of the entire movie. And they have this place, in England, near Orvane. It's the edge of the world. Beyond the edge. A four mile spit of shingle jutting into the North Sea. Water on both sides and the sky pressing down. This spit of shingle is shaped like a hook. They say it migrates eight inches to the west every year. It's alive, David! Imagine it, the landscape creeping across the map. In this place the sky weighs more, the light is liquid. Unfenced existence, they call it. We must have Orvane. Fair Orvane! And we must have Spurn Head. Without it my vision will be incomplete. Without it there will be a vacuum at the heart of this movie. A black hole that will suck the very life out of the movie and anyone who watches it. Without Orvane the entire movie will be a disaster. It will be a tragedy.'

'Anna?' asks Campanile.

Anna sighs. It's the same every time. Sal's artistic incontinence and Campanile's predictable unpredictability. And Anna Sampson's unchanging advice, thinks Anna. My advice should be chiselled in tablets of stone, she thinks. Wrought into the lintel of the building. Written in the deep blue air by one of those aerobatic biplanes trailing smoke.

'Do nothing,' she says. 'That will show them where the power lies.'

Campanile says, 'There's no power in doing nothing, Anna. Didn't they teach you anything at law school?'

Anna says nothing.

'Say something, Anna. You're making me nervous.'

Anna extends the silence.

'Anna? I need to know. Please don't make me say please.'

A beat.

'My advice remains,' says Anna. 'Do nothing.'

'Increase the offer,' says Campanile.

'Do nothing.'

'Now,' says Campanile.

'No.'

'It's my money, Anna, and I'm telling you to offer them more of it. I can always find another attorney.'

'But you never do,' says Anna.

Her phone pings. She extracts it from the inside pocket of her jacket.

She says, 'It's Fullerton-Bagshawe. They accept.'

3

The south is a foreign country, thinks Jonty. They do things differently there.

He keeps his eyes on the road, his hands upon the wheel. It's been an early start. He's returning north after late-night negotiations near Maidenhead.

Abruptly the landscape flattens and the sky widens and he feels the broad ribbon of the M18 begin to reel him in.

The road accepts him home in a way that Oliver never will. In Oliver Mundayne's eyes Jonty will always be an offcumden, despite having lived four-fifths of his life in God's own county. Despite he and Oliver having boarded together at St Peter's and spent their half term breaks together at Orvane. Despite the Earl and Countess inviting him as a matter of course to family occasions and treating him more as a favoured cousin than merely Oliver's school friend. Despite - or perhaps because of - the Earl and Countess treating him as one of their own, even paying his fees for sixth form after his father walked out.

Bloody southerner.

The words stung, and still do. Is that what Oliver really thinks, deep down? There's no balm for that - not even an entire night of negotiating near Maidenhead. Not even two nights of negotiating near Maidenhead.

Swerving east, away from the rich industrial shadows of Ferrybridge and Drax, the M18 becomes the M62, running now between thin and thistled fields and into the morning sun. The sudden glare, diffused by the insect-spattered windscreen, is like a net curtain dropped over the car. It's nigh-on impossible to see the road.

Shit, mutters Jonty.

He yanks at the screen-wash stub on the steering column but the reservoir is empty. The dry wipers judder as they drag the insect spatters into smudges and smears and streaks. The degree of impossibility in seeing the road escalates from nigh-on to total.

Shit, says Jonty again. His phone pings. Shit.

He reaches for his water bottle, stabs his finger at the window control and leans out to douse the screen. The steering wheel moves with him, triggering a rhythmic rumble of low-profile tyres on cat's eyes. He's veering into the middle lane. Shit. A horn blares. He adjusts the wheel with his left hand, thumbs open the sports cap of the water bottle with his right and squeezes. His slipstream pelts him with expensive gobbets of Pyrenean mountain water. Thankfully, enough of it reaches the screen for the wipers to gain purchase. His vision is restored. Thank God for the over-priced fridges of Watford Gap. He swigs the last of the mineral water and tosses the empty bottle into the passenger footwell.

He's closing in on a green-liveried road train. Eddie Stobart. He remembers the ping and glances down at his phone. New message from Anna Sampson.

Sampson will have to wait.

He checks the mirror, moves out to overtake the truck and everything changes. Ahead, the haunches of the Ouse Bridge rise out of the plain of Inclesmoor. Moments later the bridge is bearing him skywards. From the apex, over the parapet, stands the muscular profile of Howden Minster. The tower is sharp-edged in the morning sun, etched against the deep blue sky as if it's just unfolded itself miraculously from the freshly opened page of a pop-up story book.

Here, thinks Jonty. Here I am.

The moment fizzes with significance. There will never be another like it. The conjunction of the sun, the bridge, the Minster, his car. He's acutely aware of himself: his feet on the pedals, his hands on the wheel, his place in the universe - a speck in a system. Perhaps it's the adrenalin; his near-miss. Perhaps it's the elevation. He savours the moment; the pause between cosmic breaths. Then it's gone and he's descending the long slide down the far arc of the bridge, back down to earth, where engineering relinquishes the road once more to the landscape.

He slows for the junction. Eddie Stobart overhauls him and rumbles past, Hull-bound. Then he's climbing the exit ramp and leaving the motorway behind him.

Here, at Howden, with the Minster as his pivot, he'll change course; set a new bearing. From here he'll cut a diagonal north-east across the map; light out homeward over the undulating chalk of the Wolds, unrolling in waves, fold upon fold upon fold, dark-dotted with isolate stands of trees.

Howden, Market Weighton, Wetwang, Foxholes. Now the final climb into Eoferwic How.

Jonty slows as he approaches. It is a homecoming, he thinks, whatever Oliver might say. And it deserves its place on the map: five times winner of Yorkshire In Bloom and seven times winner of the East Riding Scarecrow Festival.

He passes the sign, mounted on a disc of sandstone at the edge of the town: Eoferwic How. Everwick, he thinks. Everwick Hill. Why the ancient spelling? To confuse the enemy in the event of an invasion?

Oliver's ancestors have insinuated their sense of self into the fabric of the settlement that shares their title; into the fabric of the town-on-the-hill that once marked the heart of the Mundayne Earldom and now constitutes the extent of it. They've marked their territory. Merged themselves with it. Spliced themselves into it, so that the histories of Eoferwic How and the Earls of Eoferwic are inseparable.

The Norman church, to Jonty's right as he drives through the town, is filled with alabaster effigies of Mundayne grandees and marble memorials to Mundayne achievements. The squat stone tower is adorned on all four faces with the Mundayne coat of arms. The tower is topped not with a crucifix but with a Mundayne weather vane that turns with the wind, just as the Mundaynes did in the civil war.

On the other side of the road from the church, on Jonty's left as he rounds the bend, is Orvane Hall. A stream runs beside the road, delineating the boundary of the estate. Jonty brakes, negotiates the roughstone bridge

19

over the stream and passes between the twin gatehouses into the grounds.

Glancing up at the sculpted wild boar, one on each gatehouse roof, he loses himself in a strange combination of anticipation and nostalgia, a feeling familiar since childhood.

The approach to the Hall is still breathtaking, even after all these years. A two-mile lime-lined avenue zeroes in on the magnificent Smythson facade. Framed by the twin rows of trees, Orvane is a doll's house; a perfect scale model of itself. The arrow-straight avenue - known, appropriately, as The Avenue - calls for stately progress. As always, Jonty carefully observes the 5mph speed limit and, as always, he curses the effect the speed bumps nonetheless have on his sports suspension and his coccyx. He worries whether the repeated jarring of his undercarriage will affect his ability to negotiate next time he's near Maidenhead.

The Hall hoves closer.

As does his meeting with the Earl.

On the back seat are the tools of his trade: suit, tie and briefcase - the instruments of persuasion. He tries to manifest the meeting - to prepare himself, mentally - but the repeated sameness of the trees gliding towards the car and receding in the mirror is hypnotic. First he feels he's continuously passing between the same pair of trees, moving but going nowhere; then that he's stopped moving and the Hall is rolling towards him, expanding as it approaches, looming ever larger as it makes the transition from replica to reality.

4

Thirty-three storeys above the streets of Los Angeles, spotlit at the centre of the conference table, sits a perfect scale model of Orvane.

It's a world of its own. An exercise in reality and unreality. Precise in every detail yet with no nod to naturalism. The fearful symmetry of Smythson's architecture is rendered in three dimensions but the modellers' card is virgin-white and the peripheral details are flat.

There are scant pencilled embellishments - pencilled diamond-leading for the windows; pencilled eyes and tusks for the two-dimensional wild boar on the gatehouse roofs; pencilled curlicues for the leaves on the two-dimensional trees that line The Avenue.

Parked at an angle to the semi-circular portico is a white card car with pencilled smears obscuring the windscreen. Beside the car is a white card figure holding a white card suit bag and a white card briefcase. The figure is leaning towards the car, free hand on the open driver's door, about to swing it closed and climb the semi-circular steps of the Hall to some imagined meeting.

Grouped round the model, generals in a war-room leaning fatefully over the map-table, are the senior members of Belltower Studios' production team. Leading the discussion, explaining her model, is the production designer, Simone Rogers.

'Magnificent!' exclaims Campanile.

Anna Sampson raises an eyebrow. Enthusiasm from Campanile is rare. She glances at him and sees his exclamation is directed not at Simone's model but at whatever has just popped up on his phone.

'What's this?' asks Sal, brandishing a pencil like a miniature swagger stick. 'A car? A suit? The car and the suit must go, Simone! The car and the suit are anachronisms. There will be no cars or suits in my movie. There will be no briefcases.'

Simone takes a deep breath. The call came six weeks ago. Belltower wanted an English production designer - someone raised in the land of the Bard; someone steeped in the English architectural vernacular. Simone's agent assured Belltower that Simone is England's best and Simone's agent assured Simone that Hollywood is a good career move. But Hollywood remains a white sign on the distant hills, barely visible through the window over Campanile's shoulder, half-obscured by heat-haze and smog. And communicating in the American vernacular is proving problematic.

Simone exhales.

'The car and the mannequin,' she explains, 'are not obligatory. They're not part of the setting. They're there to give a sense of scale.'

'Not part of the setting? Then they must be removed. Removed!' Sal swipes at the mannequin with his swagger stick.

The figure remains firmly fixed.

Simone smiles. 'Two-part epoxy.'

'Unnecessary and anachronistic.' Sal swipes again.

The figure drops his briefcase but remains standing.

'And obstinate. There will be no obstinacy in my movie. There will be no anachronisms. The scale is obvious from the redwoods.'

'They're not - '

'Wait!' Sal narrows his eyes. He tilts his head. He taps his pencil on his teeth. He says, 'It's smaller than I remember.'

'That's because they're not redwoods,' says Simone. 'The mannequin is the scale reference.'

'Not redwoods?'

'They're lime trees.'

'Lime trees. So it's bigger than it looks?'

Anna sighs. It's the same every time. Campanile's inability to enthuse and Sal's inability to see what's in front of him.

Simone says, 'It's fifty times bigger than the model.'

Campanile glances up from his phone. 'Show me where we park the catering wagons. Talking of which' - his gaze scans the room for his PA - 'ah, there you are, Gregory. Coffee, please. Eighty-eight degrees. Unsweetened almond milk, MCT oil, no sugar. Coffee, Simon?'

'Simone,' says Simone. 'As in Nina. Yes, please. Black.'

'Gregory, you heard the lady,' says Campanile. 'Now, these trees. How big are they?'

23

Anna rolls her eyes.

'The mannequin is there to show how big everything is,' says Simone. 'The mannequin is a point of reference we can all relate to. In many ways the mannequin is the north star.'

'I don't want to hear about astrology,' says Campanile. 'I want to hear about trees.'

'It's a phrase,' says Simone. 'The pole star. A way of getting your bearings. A lodestone, if you like. The compass needle points towards it, the heavens revolve around it - it's the star at the centre of it all.'

From beyond the open doorway of the conference room comes a voice. 'How now, who calls?'

Everyone looks up.

Izzie Markham materialises in the doorway. She pauses for effect, then sweeps into the room.

Her entourage follows.

'Now that is what I call a welcome!' gushes Izzie. 'The star at the centre of it all!'

She stops mid-way between the door and the conference table. Her entourage stops too. She raises both hands, takes an exaggerated gasp. 'And this must be Simone!' she exclaims. 'Oh beauteous flower!'

Simone is unsure whether she's being flattered or patronised.

'I *love* your British accent,' continues Izzie. 'Say that again - about the star.'

Simone looks round the conference table. Is she being set up? She repeats, 'The star at the centre of it all.'

Izzie repeats her response: 'How now, who calls?'

She says, 'See what I did there, Sal? That's Juliet's first line.'

Simone considers the bundle of conflicting signals that has entered the room. Dark hair, dark eyes, dark dress. A study in darkness. And yet the room is brighter, more spacious. Izzie's darkness intensifies the light around her. Her corona draws everyone's gaze. Time is suspended. Izzie alone can break the spell.

Without a word Izzie takes two more steps towards the conference table. Her entourage does the same.

The big screen made her a star, thinks Simone, but even at 1:1 scale she looks like a star. No, not 'Looks.' She emanates stardom. Only nineteen but wearing the mantle of fame like it's made-to-measure.

'*Look* at *this*!' Izzie raises her hands to Simone's model the way she did to Simone. 'Is this fair Verona, where we lay our scene?'

Without awaiting an answer Izzie rounds the conference table and leans in close to wonder at the model.

'Where's my balcony?'

'Here! Here it is! It's perfect!'

She puts her right hand on her heart, extends her left, gazes out into the deep blue air and declaims, 'O Romeo, Romeo! Wherefore art thou Romeo? Deny thy father and refuse thy name. Or, if thou wilt not, be but sworn my love and I'll no longer be a Capulet.'

She strikes a pose. She flexes infinitesimally at the waist to symbolise a bow. Her entourage applauds, led by Brooke Laddie and 'AJ' Glass - Izzie's ever-faithful agent and her ever-enthusiastic PA.

Simone thinks, Why the need for this heavily-rehearsed grand entrance? What is she trying to prove and who is she trying to prove it to? Perhaps that's how it works, the maintenance of stardom. Stars shine all

25

day, after all, even if we only see them at night. Today Izzie is playing a star arriving for a production meeting. Tomorrow she will be playing someone else doing something else. Like Simone's model, a blank canvas. She watches AJ conjure up a chair and place it behind Izzie as she sits.

'So,' asks Izzie. 'Where is Romeo?'

'Late,' says Sal.

'Tardiness,' observes Brooke, 'is the only thing Nicolas Earl has left in his arsenal.'

'Brooke!' Izzie's voice denotes disapproval but her eyes denote delight.

Brooke nods at the open doorway. 'Speak of the devil.'

A woman has appeared. Earl's agent, Ellen Port.

Brooke smiles at his counterpart. 'Hello Ellen. Where is Mr Earl? Powdering his nose?'

'Hi again everyone!' says Ellen. 'Hi, hi! Nick will be with us any moment. My, that elevator is fast. It made my ears pop! David, do you have water? I need to swallow something. Thank you, Gregory. Now,' says Ellen - taking her place at the table while Gregory brings chilled Pyrenean mountain water and a glass with ice and two slices of cucumber - 'billing.'

'Ellen, we've discussed billing,' says Campanile. 'The subject is closed.'

'Nick was, erm, indisposed,' says Ellen. 'Now he's had time to consider. The subject needs to be reopened.'

'My client is the star of this movie,' says Brooke. 'My client has first billing.'

'The movie is Romeo and Juliet,' says Ellen. 'Romeo is the star. Nicolas Earl's name comes first.'

Anna says, 'Children, please. This isn't a haggling matter. There are rules of precedence.'

'Exactly,' says Brooke. 'Izzie is bigger box office.'

'Nick is established.'

'Established?' says Brooke. 'We all know what that means. Come on Ellen, you can do better than that.'

'Face it, Ellen,' says Campanile. 'Nick needs Izzie more than Izzie needs Nick.'

Ellen gives Campanile her best stare. She says, 'Nick and Izzie are both alike in dignity. Izzie is only who she is because of Nick.'

Campanile holds her gaze. 'Only one of them is on the way up, Ellen. Izzie gets first billing. I can always find another Romeo.'

'Alright, already. But Nick goes on the left of the artwork.'

Brooke says, 'No way! Romeo on the balcony? Juliet looking up?'

'That's not what I said, Brooke, and you know it.'

'The balcony is always on the left. And Juliet is always on the balcony.'

Sal bangs his fist on the conference table. 'My movie is not about balconies! There will be no balconies on the artwork. My movie is about ancient grudges and new mutiny. It is about star-cross'd lovers and piteous overthrows. It is about death-marked love and the discontinuance of rage.'

Sal ends as abruptly as he began.

Into the silence Izzie says, 'See, where he comes.'

Nick is standing in the doorway, dazzled by sudden sunlight.

'Morning Nick,' says Brooke.

Nick sniffs. He says, 'Is the day so young?'

5

'A film?' booms the Earl. 'What sort of film?'

'Shakespeare,' says Jonty. 'Romeo and Juliet.'

There's trepidation in his voice. The Earl is an imposing figure, despite his illness, and selling faits accompli is not one of the tricks Jonty learned in law school.

He adjusts his tie.

'It's a necessary evil,' says Oliver, too loud and too fast. He doesn't like having to defend what he previously opposed.

'You mean we'll have luvvies trampling all over the estate?' booms the Earl. 'RSC types declaiming everywhere?'

'Our C-types?'

'Not everything is about the bike collection, Jonty, marvellous though the bike collection may be. You need to learn how to listen, lad. I said R – S – C. The Royal Shakespeare Company. Didn't they teach you two anything at St Peter's? What the hummer did I pay all those fees for? Remind me to ask for a refund.'

'There won't be any RSC types,' says Jonty. 'They're American. Izzie Markham is Juliet.'

'Who is Lizzie Markham?'

'Izzie,' says Jonty.

Jonty has done his research. He knows which buttons to press.

'She was Catherine,' he says, 'in that adaptation of *Wuthering Heights* you and Lady Mundayne liked.'

He puts his briefcase on the desk, clicks the clasps and extracts a laminated A4 reproduction of the *Wuthering Heights* billboard poster. He holds it up for the Earl and Countess to see.

The Earl raises an eyebrow.

Beyond the diamond-leaded windows winter comes to an end.

Spring begins.

Oliver draws breath to speak but Jonty forestalls him with a gesture.

Somewhere in the Hall a cuckoo clock sounds.

The Earl reaches a decision.

'Izzie Markham a necessary evil? Oliver, what are you on about, lad? Necessary evil pisshh. It's a marvellous idea. Marvellous. Well done, Jonty. Just what this place needs. Where do I sign?'

Oliver says, 'We've already - '

Jonty cuts him off with another gesture. He puts the poster back in the briefcase and extracts an unsigned copy of the contract.

'Here,' says Jonty. He puts the contract on the desk, slides it towards the Earl and proffers the Mont Blanc.

At the foot of the last page is a yellow sticker with the words SIGN HERE beside a red hand, forefinger extended towards the signature block.

The Earl signs.

'Good man,' he says, handing back the pen. He doesn't register it as the pen he and Lady Mundayne gave Jonty for his 21st, just as he didn't register the briefcase as the one he and Lady Mundayne gave Jonty for his 18th.

'Just what the place needs,' says the Earl again. 'Eh, Oliver? Initiative. Gumption. Fresh ideas.'

Oliver says nothing.

'That's what it's about, lad. Character. Strong characters make things happen. The weak get swept along with the tide. Jonty is making things happen. Yes. It'll be like the War all over again. All those Yanks marching round the estate. I remember following them round in my buckled shoes and short trousers, marching in step with a yard-brush at slope arms. Escape and evasion in the spinney. Throwing pine cone hand grenades from the cover of the trees.'

A coughing fit reminds them all that behind the booming voice and the imposing frame the Earl is frail.

When he gets his breath back he says, 'Those were the days! We showed those Yanks a thing or two about how to fight a war.'

'It would be politic not to refer to our guests as Yanks,' says Jonty.

'Why ever not, lad? Why ever not?'

'Etiquette,' says Jonty.

'But that's what they are, isn't it? Yanks? You said so yourself, Jonty.'

'I said they're American,' says Jonty.

'Same thing, isn't it?'

'It's complicated,' says Jonty. 'They have a north-south divide.'

'We can teach them a thing or two about north-south divides,' booms the Earl. 'Will there be Nissen huts?'

'Winnebagos,' says Jonty.

'And what about the NAAFI? And the convoys?'

'There will be catering,' says Jonty. He pats the contract with the flat of his hand. 'It's all in here. Catering and convoys. Lots of trucks. But no new roads or runways or radar stations.'

'Damned right,' says the Earl. 'We're still tripping over chunks of the last lot. Concrete everywhere. Did you have Yanks at Allerton, Olivia? In the War?'

'Ours were Canadian,' says Lady Mundayne. 'The airfield was on the way to school. 443 Squadron. They were known as the Maple Leafs.' She smiles at the memory.

'Leaves, Olivia, surely?'

'Leafs,' says Lady Mundayne. 'That's what it said on their... what-do-you-call-it? Insignia.'

'If you say so, darling. Those were the days. Marvellous. Even if we did have to retreat to the East Wing for the duration.'

Plus ça change, thinks Oliver. The Mundaynes have once again retreated to the East Wing. They're exiles in their own home. Creeping through the servants' passageways if they want to visit the public part of the Hall. And not due to wartime requisitions, this time. This time it's financial - and irreversible. The better part of their home is a museum.

A museum of what, though? thinks Oliver. Lost times. We're curators of our own past. There's plenty to curate: the Norman manor house and church, the Elizabethan Hall, the Georgian furniture. The renaissance paintings, the Victorian follies, the modern sculptures. For a few weeks in summer it's busy - they've had to tarmac over the orchard for overflow parking - but a few weeks isn't enough, and people don't come for all that. They come for the albino peacocks and the Jaconelli ice cream franchise and Mandy Howe's jungle-themed gift shop. They spend longer contemplating the bouncy castle than the Hockneys. Children climb on the Henry Moore.

A question from the Earl brings Oliver back to the room.

'So, Jonty. Have you found Oliver a wife yet?'

'Marmaduke!' says Lady Mundayne. 'Don't be indelicate. You'll embarrass the poor lad. It's not Jonty's responsibility.'

'Somebody's got to take responsibility,' says the Earl. 'No point him becoming 13th Earl if he can't produce an heir. I haven't got long left. Before I shuffle off this mortal coil I'd like to know there's an heir on the way. Someone to continue the line.' He turns to Oliver. 'What happened to that lass Rosaline from Foxholes? Nowt wrong with her.'

'She wasn't interested,' says Oliver. 'Not in me, anyway.' He glances at Jonty.

Jonty looks away.

'What about this Lizzie Markham, then?'

'Izzie,' says Oliver.

That's... improbable, thinks Jonty. He keeps the thought to himself. Instead he says, 'Nicolas Earl might have something to say about that.'

'Who?' booms the Earl.

'Heathcliff,' says Jonty. 'And Romeo.'

'What about Nicolas Earl, then, if he's such a romantic hero?' says the Earl. 'An Earl for an Earl.'

'Marmaduke!'

'Why not?' says the Earl. 'It's nothing new. Been going on since the ancient Greeks. They could adopt.'

Jonty says, 'According to the gossip columns Izzie Markham and Nicolas Earl will be more interested in each other. They were spotted together in a hotel foyer after an awards ceremony. A photographer was lurking behind a plastic plant.'

'Heathcliff was trouble,' says Oliver. 'A usurper. Hardly a hero.'

'Gossip columns?' says the Earl. 'About as reliable as the weather forecast. Cloud-cuckoo stuff. You never know what might happen. So. When's D-Day? When does the invasion begin?'

'Twenty-third of April,' says Jonty.

'St George's Day,' observes the Earl.

'Shakespeare's birthday,' says Oliver. 'You know he died on the same day?'

The Earl says, 'A bit sudden, isn't it, Jonty? We've only just signed the contract. A bit rash? I hope we're going to have some joy out of it.'

'Not the same day, obviously,' says Oliver. 'He couldn't have written all those plays. Same date, different year.'

'Not long to prepare,' continues the Earl. 'Only a month.'

'Thirty-three days,' says Jonty. 'Plenty of time.'

'That's the spirit!' booms the Earl. 'But haven't they left it a bit late, Jonty, these Yanks? The signature? A bit last minute. Just like the War.'

Oliver says, 'When well-appareled April on the heel of limping winter treads.'

'Just make sure everything is in place at our end, Jonty,' says the Earl. 'We'll show them a thing or two about making films.'

Jonty, relieved, takes that as his cue to leave. He stands and nods at Oliver to do the same.

Lady Mundayne stays them with a question. 'Jonty,' she says. 'Why are they filming it here? Isn't it supposed to be in Italy?'

Before Jonty can say anything the Earl booms out an answer. 'Because Yorkshire is a continent unto itself, Olivia. Because God's own county is all things to all men. Even Yanks.'

6

Yeadon Airport is shrouded in mist.

Campanile stifles a yawn.

Sal says, 'The faster you travel the longer it takes to catch up with yourself.'

'Says who?'

'They,' says Sal. 'Them. They say it, David. The faster you travel the more separate you become. Breakfast?'

Campanile nods.

The advance party - Campanile, Sal and Gregory - is passing through a food zone. Suitcases are stacked precariously on a low trolley with a wonky wheel. Sal and Campanile walk ahead, Gregory follows. Gregory's back is twisted. His wrist and forearm ache. His knee is beginning to bulge. Keeping the trolley on course is harder work than keeping Campanile on course. The wonky wheel wants to go its own way.

'It makes sense,' continues Sal. 'We're designed for walking. Or running, I suppose. When we stuck to walking or running we never got ahead of ourselves.'

'We?'

'Us,' says Sal. 'Humans. Then we started riding horses. That wasn't too bad. Have you ever ridden a horse, David? It's good for your core stability. For balance. But then came engines. Trains and cars and planes. We're not designed for that. It goes against nature. That's why fatigue increases with speed. It's directly proportional.'

'Nothing to do with the hours of inactivity?' says Campanile. 'The missed sleep, the forced air, the crossing of time zones? The tedious transfers at featureless hubs. The proliferation of abbreviations. LAX-LHR-LBA. What does that even mean?'

'Los Angeles, London, Leeds-Bradford,' says Gregory.

'I know what it means, Gregory. What I mean is what does it *mean*? It must *mean* something. I don't want to know what it means, I want to know what it *means*.'

Sal says, 'The circles of L.'

'What?'

'Our spirit gets left behind,' says Sal. 'It can't keep up. We have to make time for it to catch up. We have to make time to reacquaint ourselves with ourselves. We have to ground ourselves. Take off your shoes, David. Feel the floor. Reconnect.'

Campanile sees Sal is barefoot. 'Reconnect? With what?

'With the earth, David. With the earth.'

'Through all this concrete and steel and hardcore and ballast? Through all these zones and levels and floors and foundations?'

'Why so literal, David? Always so *literal*. Flying separates us from ourselves. We have to reintegrate.'

'Reintegrate. Right. What if you're a pilot and you meet yourself coming back the other way?'

'That's not how it works, David.'

'So how does it work?'

'I don't know,' says Sal. Something to do with telomeres.'

The food zone is on a mezzanine. Gregory has found a small table by a large window. The window is blank. A greyish-white wall of mist presses against the glass. Out there is where the runways should be. Occasionally there's a sense of sound and speed - a swirling disturbance in the greyish-white. Planes are still arriving and departing.

A waitress takes their orders.

'Gregory,' says Campanile. 'Call Anna. I don't like this mist. It's like breakfast in purgatory.'

'Anna doesn't control the weather, David.'

'She can tell us when it will lift. Tell her Sal needs to know when his sense of self will be restored.'

'Anna will be asleep,' says Gregory. He looks at his phone. 'According to this it's sunny in Foxholes.'

Campanile ponders the possible connotations of the word. Natural. Military. Obscene. He says, 'What is Foxholes?'

'It's the nearest pronounceable place to where we're going.'

Campanile grunts.

The waitress arrives with their coffees. She slides them across the table and there's another perturbation in the static beyond the window. Campanile presses his fingers against the glass. The waitress turns and walks away and the three men slurp their drinks, scalding their mouths.

37

'Look at this,' says Campanile.

Sal turns. 'Look at what?'

'This coffee. The way it asserts its being. The way it exists, in time and space, cup-shaped within the cup. It's profound. The mist makes it profound.'

'It's coffee, David.'

'Don't spoil my existential moment, Sal. This is the essence of being, right here, in this very cup. In my very hand. I'm communing with my spirit. It just caught up. It emerged from the mist. Through the glass.'

'David, are you mocking me?'

Campanile says, 'Gregory, where are we?'

'In transit.'

Sal says, 'Gloria mundi.'

'In transit where, Gregory? I want to know where. I don't want to hear that we're part way. I don't want to hear that we're somewhere between here and there. I want specifics.'

Gregory looks again at his phone. 'Between - '

'Specifics, Gregory. I don't want 'between'.'

'Yeadon Airport,' says Gregory. 'Also known as Leeds-Bradford. The food zone.'

'I know that,' says Campanile. 'Where is Leeds-Bradford?'

'Between Leeds and Bradford.'

The waitress arrives with three breakfasts. She slides the plates across the table and turns and walks away. The three men reach for colour-coded sauces in unopenable sachets.

Campanile forks an over-fried mushroom and presses it into his egg until the yolk bursts. He watches the slow flow of golden-yellow. He says, 'Gregory, where are Simone and Julian? They're supposed to be meeting us.'

'Not here,' says Gregory. 'At the location.'

'And the rest of the crew?'

'Monday.'

Sal looks up from his breakfast. 'Who is Julian?'

'Location manager,' says Gregory.

Sal's fork stops part way to his mouth. 'Frisco is the location manager. What happened to Frisco?'

'Frisco didn't want to be on another continent,' says Campanile. 'He's a recent father.'

'Frisco is vital. Vital! I cannot make my movie without Frisco.'

'Julian works with Simone,' says Campanile. 'He's British. He understands the class system.'

'We don't need a genealogist, David. We need a location manager.'

'Julian is a location manager. He'll know how to handle the Earls. How to manage their fiefdom, Earldom, whatever these people call these things. And it's not your movie.'

'Frisco is part of the team,' says Sal. 'Part of *our* team, David. Part of the ethos. This is a bad omen. My God! We've only just arrived and already things are falling apart.'

'We haven't arrived,' says Campanile.

'We're here, aren't we?'

'Here,' says Campanile, gesturing at the blank window, 'is nowhere. We're in transit. According to Gregory we're 'between'.'

Campanile lifts a forkful of black pudding to his mouth and makes a face. He puts down the fork, still loaded, pushes away his plate and asks, 'Gregory, is breakfast scheduled?'

'Breakfast is not scheduled,' says Gregory. 'You yawned and we deviated from the schedule.'

Campanile gulps the last of his coffee. 'Where's the limo?'

'It's an MPV,' says Gregory.

Sal crosses himself. 'Oh my God.'

'An MPV is more practical,' says Gregory. 'There are rolling hills. Tight curves. Steep gradients. It's a Voyager. It has reclining leather armchairs and tinted glass. It's at Arrivals.'

'And where are we?' asks Campanile.

'Departures,' says Gregory.

'Why? How?' asks Campanile. 'I need to know. We landed. How are we not in Arrivals?'

'Breakfast brought us here,' says Gregory. 'Your yawn.'

'We were drawn by the food zone,' says Sal. 'And by the retail outlets. We were drawn by the promise of over-specced cameras and unattainable scents and extravagantly-peated whiskies. By photography and pheromones and phenols.'

Campanile says, 'Call Anna.'

7

'We've arrived.'

No response.

Gregory twists in the passenger seat of the Voyager. Behind him, Sal and Campanile are asleep in the reclining leather armchairs.

Gregory locates his phone and types a message.

Campanile's phone pings.

Campanile wakes, reads the message, looks at Gregory. 'Arrived where?'

'Here,' says Gregory.

'Here is meaningless, Gregory. *Arrived* is meaningless. Without context they're meaningless concepts.'

Campanile stares at his screen. He wakes Sal, shows him the screen.

'Look. According to Gregory we've arrived. But there's no context. Information with no context is no information at all. I want specifics, Gregory. I need to know, precisely, where we are. I don't want *here*.'

Sal gestures at the grand facade beyond the windows. 'Look outside yourself, David. You never look outside yourself. Why so internal? You're always so *internal*. We're here. Precisely here. Fair Orvane, where we lay our scene!'

Campanile presses his fingers against the tinted glass.

Simone and Julian amble towards the Voyager. The synchronised scrunch of their footfall in the gravel makes Orvane sound more opulent than the reality. A third person - the Mundaynes' estate manager - maintains a discreet distance. He remains by the semi-circular steps of the portico, squinting in the spring sunshine.

Campanile steps out of the sliding side door of the vehicle and gazes upward. 'A castle? You didn't tell me I'm paying for a castle.'

The estate manager, from his discreet distance, rolls his eyes.

Sal emerges. 'I told you there was a castle, David. You never listen.' He stretches his arms. 'We sat in your shiny meeting room in the sky and I told you there's a castle and a balcony and a church. I described them to you. Look, there's the church spire.'

Campanile looks. 'That's not a spire. It's square.'

'Late Norman,' says Simone.

Campanile says, 'What's that on top?

'A weather vane,' says Julian. 'It's a Mundayne boar.'

Campanile grunts.

'From the family crest. Hi, I'm Julian.' Julian extends his hand.

'David Campanile,' says Campanile. He extends his hand in turn. 'This is Masuccio Salernitano.'

'Sal,' says Sal.

'And this is Gregory,' says Simone to Julian. Then, to the others, 'It's not a castle, by the way.'

'Not a castle?' says Sal.

'What about the' - Campanile waves his hand upward - 'battlements?'

'Crenellations,' says Simone. 'They're an affectation. Set dressing, if you like.'

Sal says, 'The fortifications are not real?'

'They're real,' says Simone, 'but they're not fortifications.'

'Not fortifications. So Orvane is an illusion.' Sal reassesses his location. 'An illusion.' He raises a hand to cross himself, then stops. He decides an illusion is a good thing.

'The architectural term is sham,' says Simone. 'Smythson was a master of sham. In many ways Orvane is his finest.'

'A sham,' says Sal.

'Show me the balcony,' says Campanile. 'I want to see the balcony.'

The five of them scrunch westward. The estate manager adopts a converging course, and when their paths meet Simone introduces him as Abram Singleton.

'Abram, they'd like to see the West Balcony.'

'Aye,' says Abram. With a gesture he shepherds the party across the front of the Hall. They round the end of the building and assemble in front of the West Wing.

'Bellissimo!' says Sal. 'Even more beautiful than I remembered. The light. The elevation. The aspect. Perfect! David, I told you not to despair. At the airport you were ready to despair, you said it was all falling apart and I said - I told you - things will improve. They will get better, I said. And look. This is perfect. Perfect!'

43

He takes a few paces backward and nods. Then a few more. He nods again. He turns his back on the balcony, strides out a long shot, counting his exaggerated paces, and turns to face the Hall again.

He glances right and left and then ahead at the balcony. Consternation crosses his face.

He forms two 'L's with his forefingers and thumbs, reverses one of the 'L's and joins them - right forefinger to left thumb, right thumb to left forefinger - to form a widescreen frame. He raises the frame to his face, closes one eye and scrutinises his shot.

'This is wrong. Wrong! This tree. What is it, an oak? It cannot be here. The balance. It's ruined. Ruined! It will be a blight on my entire movie. Why did this have to happen? Why did this tree have to appear? When everything was going so well.'

Simone walks to where Sal is standing.

She makes a show of creating her own fingers-and-thumbs frame and looking through it. 'I see what you mean,' she says. Then, taking three steps to the side, 'What about shooting from here? From here the tree is out of shot.'

'No! No. No, no, no. The long shot must be from here. From this very spot. The golden ratio, Simone. This is why you are the designer and I am the director. This is not about the setting. This is about the shot. The setting is nothing without the shot. Nothing! It's about the angle. The golden ratio. The balcony must be shot from here. I will not have my shots dictated by trees. I will not have my vision foiled by foliage. The tree must be moved. Four feet will suffice.'

Campanile and Julian join them.

Simone looks at Julian for support. She says, 'Sal, I - '

44

'No.' He cuts her off with a gesture.

Julian begins, 'Sal, I'm not sure - '

'No!' Another gesture.

They turn to Campanile.

Campanile turns to Gregory. 'Call Anna. Ask her what the contract says about trees.'

Abram says, 'What's up?'

Everyone has forgotten Abram. All heads turn towards him. Sal begins a gesture, draws breath to say No, but he's disarmed by Abram's manner.

Into the silence Abram says, 'No point mithering about a tree. We'll sort it out.'

Simone and Julian look at him in astonishment.

Campanile nods.

Abram looks at Sal. 'When do you want it shifted?'

'Now,' says Sal.

'Now?'

'Tomorrow, then.'

Julian says, 'We're not filming the balcony scene for two weeks.'

'Julian, Julian, Julian. This is why you are the location manager and I am the director. It's not about when the scene is filmed. It's about the *ambience*. It's about creating the right feel. The right working environment. I cannot have people walking past this balcony while this tree is... misplaced. The crew arrives on Monday. St George's Day. The tree must be moved by St George's Day or the balcony scene will be ruined. And if the balcony scene is ruined my entire movie is ruined. My entire movie. The balcony scene is vital. Vital!'

'No problem,' says Abram. 'Tomorrow it is.'

'You see, David, this is what this production company needs,' says Sal. 'Initiative.'

'I take it you're staying at the Eoferwic Arms,' says Abram. 'You settle in and my lads will sort out the tree.'

'What did you say?' asks Campanile.

'My lads will sort out the tree.'

'No, the hotel,' says Campanile.

'Not hotel,' says Abram. 'Inn.'

'The name,' says Campanile. 'What did you say it's called?'

'It's pronounced 'Everwick',' says Abram. 'Like the Earl.'

They stroll back to the vehicles.

Campanile says, 'Sal, I'm sure I remember a production meeting once upon a time, in my shiny meeting room in the sky, where you said 'your' movie - this movie, *my* movie - is not about the balcony.'

'Of course it's about the balcony, David. What is Romeo and Juliet without a balcony? Romeo and Juliet without a balcony would be like Hamlet without a skull. It would be Macbeth without a dagger. Lear without a blasted heath. The balcony is iconic, David. Iconic! I will not have my balcony upstaged by a tree.'

8

'Eh up.'

'Now then.'

'What are they up to?' Jonty twitches the curtain.

'Don't know,' says Oliver. 'Some sort of warm-up, it looks like.'

Below the fifth-floor window, on the West Lawn, Sal is once again lining up a shot through fingers-and-thumbs. Around him a gaggle of acolytes is doing the same. Some are lining up long shots - leaning backwards, legs extended, arms at full stretch - others are considering close-ups: half crouched, knees bent, frames close to faces. Heads tilt this way and that. Elbows flex and extend, pulling virtual focus on imagined shots.

'Looks like ante-natal yoga,' says Jonty.

'Pilates.'

'Tai Chi.'

'Capoeira.'

'Marcel Marceau.'

'Drama at St Peter's,' says Oliver. 'Modern Theatre Group. Remember JHF?'

Jonty laughs. 'You are lying on a sunny beach,' he intones. 'Your limbs are sinking slowly into the warm sand.'

'JHF,' says Oliver. 'Why no nickname? Strange, that.'

'Because he had mellifluous initials.'

'Maybe.'

Oliver looks again at the crew massing on the West Lawn below. He thinks of the myriad vehicles lined up at the front of the Hall and in the Orchard Car Park like... what? Toys on his boyhood carpet? Tanks at the border?

The day the unit arrived Oliver was watching from a high window, his dismay increasing as the endless column of vehicles rolled down The Avenue. From his high vantage he watched one of Julian's yellow-gileted assistants consulting a clipboard and guiding each vehicle into its allotted place, marshalling the forces of Belltower Studios: the vans and the trucks and the trailers and the generators; the director's Cayenne, hired for the duration from JCT 600, and the location manager's Volvo and the designer's Alfa; the Routemaster restaurant bus and the catering vans and the honey wagons and the fire tender to feed the rain machine.

The Earl had talked of an invasion and Oliver had feared a siege but in fact, thinks Oliver, since the Americans arrived the Mundaynes have enjoyed freer rein in their home than they have for decades.

The estate is closed to the public for the duration. The family can wander the West Wing unharried by the hoi polloi. Within the Hall they are once again lords of their domain, except for the few rooms earmarked for filming. Flight cases roll continually to and from these rooms, where chippies are busy laying false floors to protect the parquet, and riggers are busy rigging grids beneath the

48

crystal chandeliers and priceless plaster mouldings, and set dressers are busy dressing sets, first photographing the existing arrangement of ornaments and artefacts and paintings to ensure they're all replaced in precisely the same places when filming is over.

The Grand Ballroom is being prepared for the Capulets' old-accustomed feast, where Romeo will encounter Juliet; the Crimson Drawing Room as the antechamber where Count Paris will ask Lord Capulet for Juliet's hand; the first-floor dressing room and balcony for use as Juliet's chamber. An outbuilding is being transformed into Friar Lawrence's cell, where well-meaning plans will be laid and go awry; the Church is being readied for the doomed wedding, and the wine cellars are being converted into the Capulet vault where the star-cross'd lovers will be united forever in death.

With the public at bay, Oliver has been able to wander the corridors of his ancestral home in almost-solitude, gazing on paintings and sculptures he hasn't had the chance in years to enjoy, marvelling anew at the Pellegrini ceiling of the Great Hall and the Gibbons carvings in the Music Room.

Strangely, though, he's found himself spending more and more time in the small rooms of the servants' quarters tucked under the eaves of the upper floors, spying on the activity below.

His misgivings about the contract, his resentment at the arrival of the advance party, his dismay at the sight of the unit vehicles, have all gradually given way to fascination at the indecipherable codes and customs of filming. He's observed a lot of disposable cups, a lot of cigarette smoke and a lot of standing around. The caterers are busier than the cameras. The caterers, he's noticed, are the first to arrive and the last to leave; the cameras vice-versa. His reverie is broken by Jonty twitching the curtain.

'Nothing's happening.'

'Nothing and everything,' says Oliver. He surprises himself with his new-found knowledge. 'That's how it's done, Jonty. It's a gradual process. A process of accretion.'

Beyond Sal's inner gaggle of acolytes is an outer circle of exoterics, some lean and earnest, with collars, cords and clipboards, others pot-bellied and raucous, in cargo shorts, faded T-shirts and outsize puffa vests, belts laden with hanging fruit - rolls of tape, multi-tools, croc clips and carabiners. The whole circus is surrounded by an inexplicable amount of equipment. Curved track, straight track, dollies, cranes, tripods, lights, booms, cables, clips, clamps, reflectors, diffusers.

The Fourth Assistant Director senses scrutiny. He glances upward.

Instinctively Oliver and Jonty duck out of sight. The 4th AD is sure he's seen a pale figure at the window and wonders whether Orvane Hall is haunted. Later, over pints of Wold Top at the Eoferwic Arms, the ghostly rumours will begin.

Jonty says, 'Remember the Knocking Game?'

'Old Abram looking around like it was the Grim Reaper's death knock,' laughs Oliver. 'He was the only one who never caught us.'

'He never thought of looking above the ground floor, bless him.'

'Couldn't, with that neck,' says Oliver. 'Alas, poor Abram.'

They return to the window. Jonty tweaks the curtain to see if the coast is clear and meets the gaze of Young

Abram looking directly at them. They each raise a hand, contrite, as if Young Abram has overheard them talking about Old Abram. Young Abram - in fact, just Abram, now Old Abram has gone - acknowledges them with a nod.

'What was he so keen to talk to you about last week?' asks Oliver.

'Muck,' says Jonty. 'And brass. He wanted me to authorise some overtime. So his lads could shift some topsoil. Special request from Sal.'

'Sal? Who's she?'

'He,' says Jonty. 'The director. Seems Abram's already on nickname terms.'

'Good for him,' says Oliver. 'Why did 'Sal' want topsoil?'

'He didn't. He wanted an oak moved.'

'What the hummer?'

'Don't worry,' says Jonty. 'They didn't dig up any trees. Abram's cannier than that. Sal wanted the tree moved four feet to the west so Abram dumped a big pile of topsoil four feet to the east. Left a couple of shovels in it. When Sal came back on Monday he thought they'd dug up the tree and moved it.'

'Give over,' says Oliver. 'He fell for that?'

'He saw what he wanted to see,' says Jonty. 'Abram knows how to sell these things. He played it down. The way Abram tells it he just said it was nothing; all in a day's work. According to the location manager Sal keeps telling every man and his lad how marvellous Abram is, how he single-handedly saved the film. Apparently he's insisting Abram goes in the credits. Tree Wrangler, something like that.'

'Good for him.' Oliver watches Abram moving with ease among the crew, chatting to runners and riggers and PAs and ADs alike, sharing the occasional laugh. Abram's manner is respectful but not deferential. Dignified. He looks more authoritative than the clipboard-carriers, thinks Oliver, and more self-assured than the belt-danglers. He's more a part of this estate than I'll ever be.

There's a ripple among the acolytes, then a parting of the waves as the crew steps back to make way for someone; an impromptu guard of honour. A figure sweeps through the resulting aisle, approaches Sal, places a hand on each of his shoulders - at once bestowing affection and preventing him leaning in too close - and plants a remote kiss in the vicinity of each of Sal's cheeks.

Oliver murmurs, 'What lady is that?'

'That,' says Jonty, with the same note of proprietorial pride he'd been unable to keep out of his voice when he announced the contract all those weeks earlier, 'is Izzie Markham.'

9

Kisses over, hands still on Sal's shoulders - still keeping him in his place - Izzie asks, 'By whose direction founds't thou out this place?'

Sal, for once, is lost for words.

At last Izzie releases him. 'Seriously, Sal. How on earth did you find this place? It's perfect. Everything I dreamed it would be.'

She gestures at the balcony. 'The perfect platform for my Juliet.'

She lets her gaze sweep across the assembled crew, and waits until all eyes are back on Izzie Markham before adding, 'The only thing missing is me!'

She claps her hands twice. 'Now. This night I hold an old accustomed feast whereto I have invited many a guest such as I love. My house and welcome on your pleasure stay.'

Sal is confused.

'Drinks in my trailer,' explains Izzie. 'It's a Markham tradition, you know that. First day on location is always

Iz, fizz and physogs. Now, you still haven't spilled the beans. How did you find this place?'

Simone is within earshot so Sal has to admit, 'Our English architectural expert.'

'Simone!' gushes Izzie. 'Of course!' She conjures a piece of paper from an inner pocket and holds it aloft. 'You're top of my list, Simone.' Handing the paper to one of the runners she says, 'Peter, find everyone whose name is on this list and make sure they know where and when.'

'But soft!' says Izzie, noticing a pale face at an upper window. 'What light through yonder window breaks?'

'That'll be the Earl,' says Sal.

'Nick?' asks Izzie. 'What's he doing up there?' She raises a hand, half greeting, half dismissal. The face vanishes from the window.

'Not Nick Earl,' says Sal. '*The* Earl. The owner.'

'The Earl's son, actually,' says Julian. 'He won't be the Earl until the Earl dies. He's been watching us work. Seems to think we haven't noticed.'

'Sal, I need to ask you something important,' says Izzie. She draws Sal by the arm, away from Julian and the acolytes. 'This tree.'

'Tree?'

'Craig showed me the long shot of the balcony,' says Izzie. 'The angle's not right. My profile.' She tilts her head to one side and runs her fingers along her cheekbone. 'The angle needs to be more... what's the word? Obscure.'

'Obtuse,' says Sal.

'I knew you'd agree, Sal. Craig says the tree needs to move. Not far. Three or four feet should be enough.'

'Craig Ellachie should not be showing people my shots,' says Sal.

'People!' says Izzie. '*People*?'

54

'Even stars, Izzie darling. Even stars.' (Especially stars, he thinks.) 'This is why Craig is the cinematographer and I am the director. The shot has been carefully calibrated.'

'It needs to be recalibrated,' says Izzie. 'I can't perform until the tree is moved. Any questions, talk to Brooke. I'll be in my trailer.'

Sal does not want an argument with Brooke Laddie. As soon as Izzie is out of earshot he calls, 'Fetch Abram! I need Abram. Urgently! My movie depends on it.'

Before anyone can act on Sal's direction Abram appears. 'What's up?'

'Abram! Thank God! The tree. Izzie wants it moved. She wants it moved back to where it was before. Before you moved it. But my shot. My shot is perfect, thanks to you. The tree must stay but it must move. It must be here but it must be there.'

'Topsoil's still where we left it,' says Abram quietly, shepherding Sal still further from the acolytes' earshot. 'I'll get my lads to shift it.'

'How will that help?' asks Sal. 'You don't understand. Izzie says the shot is wrong. Her profile. She wants the tree to be moved. She's going to talk to her agent. Oh my God! We've only just started shooting and already everything is falling apart. This is a disaster. A disaster! Moving a pile of earth is not the answer. Moving the earth will not satisfy Izzie Markham.'

'My lads will move the earth,' says Abram, 'and Miss Markham will think the tree has moved.'

'How so?'

'Miss Markham will see the topsoil over there' - he points - 'and think the tree has moved to here.'

'A con?' says Sal. 'It's too obvious. Surely no one would fall for such blatant trickery?'

'Miss Markham will see what she wants to see,' says Abram.

'Abram, my movie is in your hands,' says Sal, taking one of Abram's hands in both of his. 'My career. My life! My life is in your hands! Are you sure this ruse will succeed?'

'Aye,' says Abram. 'It'll work.'

10

'Oh, she doth teach the torches to burn bright!' breathes Izzie.

Brooke is the only person to hear Izzie's observation over the background music, the chink of champagne glasses and the buzz of conversation.

The gleaming interior of Izzie's Winnebago is polished to a tee, trays of canapes are circulating, the broad tinted windows are filtering the last of a spectacular sunset and as the light drains from the sky the LED mood-lighting is beginning to take effect.

Izzie's attention is directed over Brooke's shoulder. She says, 'Beauty too rich for use, for earth too dear.'

Brooke turns and follows Izzie's gaze. Simone has arrived, fashionably late and fashionably dressed.

Izzie glides across the trailer.

'Simone! Welcome aboard!'

She takes Simone's hands in hers, pulls Simone towards her and plants a kiss on each cheek.

'Come.'

She ushers Simone through the gathering to her favoured area: the bay window of the Winnebago's rear slide-out. This zone is slightly raised and differentially lit, giving it special status.

Simone takes in the view, first inside then out. She nods at the sun dipping below the horizon. 'Julian gave you the best spot, then.'

Izzie smiles. 'Naturally. A vision for a vision! But you need a glass. Peter! Fizz for our designer, please. Your English trees are so cute.'

'Apple blossom,' says Simone. 'This part of the estate was an orchard before it was a car park.'

'Your accent!' laughs Izzie. 'Core pork! I'm loving it. How do you do that? Co-o-re po-o-rk. Alternate sayings for everything! Even parking lot.'

'These few trees are all that's left. You're lucky your trailer looks this way.'

'Not luck. Brooke makes sure I get what I deserve.'

Simone says, 'In many ways the apple is the quintessential English fruit. It's - '

Izzie puts her hand on Simone's arm. 'Forbidden,' she breathes. 'Are you ever tempted by forbidden fruit, Simone?' She holds Simone's eye. Her expression is unreadable.

Simone looks away. She's unsure whether she's being flirted with or whether Izzie is putting her down. She nods again at the horizon. 'You can see right across the Wolds.'

'The Wolds?'

'All that rolling countryside,' says Simone. 'Beyond the apple trees. Sometimes you can't see till you look through someone else's eyes. Hockney unlocks it.'

Izzie says, 'Didn't he do swimming pools?'

'When he was in California,' says Simone. 'Then he came home. Now he does fields and foliage. In many ways Hockney is to the Wolds what Wordsworth was to the Lake District.'

Izzie has already turned away. She's looking over Simone's shoulder, across the crowded trailer and through the opposite window. She leans close to Simone and nods towards Nick's trailer. 'See, where he comes.'

Nick is emerging from his Winnebago on the other side of the car park. They watch him turn to help Ellen negotiate the step.

'Late,' observes Izzie.

'I was late too,' says Simone. 'Sorry.'

'Forgiven,' says Izzie. 'You weren't trying to prove a point. Unlike Nick. Tardiness is the only thing Nick Earl has left in his arsenal.'

Brooke's phrase, thinks Simone. Has she forgotten I was there? She asks, 'What does Nick need to prove?'

'He resents second billing,' says Izzie. 'And having a smaller trailer. Mine is eight feet longer.'

Simone is unsure how to respond. 'Eight feet?'

'It's in my contract,' says Izzie. 'Eight feet longer, electric blinds and triple slide-outs. Nick has double slide-outs. His blinds are manual.'

Simone takes a canapé from a passing tray.

'These things are important,' continues Izzie, waving away the canapés. 'Here they are. Let's have some fun.' She signals Peter to bring Nick and Ellen over.

Simone feels the room shrink as Nick approaches. Now the trailer feels crowded. The volume of the chatter dips a notch.

Izzie says, 'Nick, Ellen, welcome to the pleasure dome!' She grasps Nick's shoulders, performs two perfunctory air kisses and pushes him away. Ellen receives the same treatment. 'How was your flight?'

'Turbulent,' says Nick.

'What does a gal have to do for a drink around here?'

'Oh, Ellen, darling, so sorry!' says Izzie. 'Peter! Peter! Oh, I can't seem to catch Peter's eye.'

'I'll go,' sighs Ellen. 'Nick? Bubbly?'

'Not really,' says Nick.

'To drink.'

'Oh. I see.' Nick sniffs. 'Yes, please.'

'Don't you think the apple blossom is beautiful?' says Izzie. 'I don't suppose you get the full impact from your side of the parking lot. The full splendour.'

Nick sniffs again. 'I don't do views. My blinds stay down.'

'Permanent white-out,' says Izzie. 'How apt.'

'Not white. California sunscapes.'

'Your blinds are decorated?'

'Of course,' says Nick. 'To complement the Grand Canyon on the Smeg.'

'Smeg?'

'Are you ok, Izzie?' asks Nick. 'You look as if you've seen a ghost. Talking of which, is it haunted? The castle?'

Simone nods. 'So they say. But it's not a castle.'

Nick says, 'There was a face at the window.'

'The Orvane ghost doesn't have a face,' says Simone. 'Or a head. You must have seen Oliver Mundayne.'

'Who?'

'The Earl's son.'

'You mean the tweedy buffoon who stopped me going into the castle? He's a prize asshole.' In his best English accent Nick says, 'A self-important over-bearing pompous twat.'

Izzie says, 'Careful, Nick. When you point your finger there are three more pointing back at you.'

'Standing up for the afflicted, Izzie? Not your usual style.'

Ellen returns with two flutes of champagne and Julian.

'Dizzie's fixated on the Earl,' says Nick as he accepts his glass from Ellen. 'She's got a soft spot for that fat buffoon who stopped us going into the castle when we arrived. He's been perving from the top windows.'

'Fat?' says Izzie. 'At least he's got something about him. He's a real earl, for a start.'

'Actually he's a viscount,' says Julian.

'I thought he was an earl?'

'He's the Earl's heir,' says Julian. 'Until he inherits he's just a viscount. Honorary.'

'Whatever,' says Izzie, waving away the correction. 'Still better than being a fake earl.'

She turns to Simone. 'Someone advised Nicolas Parish here that changing his name to Earl would make him sound more important. More marketable.'

Ellen has been contemplating the bubbles detaching themselves from the sides of her glass and rising through her champagne. She looks up. 'Are you having a go at me, Izzie?'

Izzie smiles. 'Not at you, Ellen. You were just doing your job.'

Nick says, 'Shall we call a truce, Izzie? After all, tomorrow we'll be lovers.' He puts his hand on her arm. 'Did my heart love till now? Forswear it, sight! For I ne'er saw true beauty till this night.'

'Get your hand off me. A fake fumble in a hotel foyer doesn't give you *rights*, Nick. That was just for the camera.'

She turns to Simone and smiles. Linking her arm through Simone's she says, 'Shall we?' Without waiting for an answer she leads Simone through the gathering to join Campanile and Sal at the ice sculpture.

At Izzie and Simone's approach Sal nods, stops talking and takes a half step away from Campanile.

'You look guilty,' says Izzie. 'Were you talking about me?'

'No,' says Sal.

'Why not?'

'Yes,' says Sal. 'We were discussing the feast.'

'Marvellous, isn't it?' says Izzie, taking a large glass and a small canapé from a passing tray.

'Not this feast,' says Sal. 'The Capulets' feast. Act one, scene five. Tomorrow's call. I've decided to invite the Earl. He's been spooking the crew so I've invited him on set. It's best if he's there in the flesh instead of peering through windows.'

'He's not an earl,' says Izzie. 'He's only a viscount. David, I have a bone to pick with you. Nick's blinds are decorated. And his fridge-freezer is a Smeg. Why do I have a Hotpoint when Nick has a Smeg?'

'There's nothing in your contract about Nick's fridge,' says Campanile. 'Anna checked.'

'And I suppose he has under-floor heating?'

'All the trailers have under-floor heating, Izzie. It comes as standard.'

'I need a Smeg, David. Urgently. I can't be Juliet without a Smeg. I need a Smeg before tomorrow's call.'

'Have Brooke sort it out with Anna,' says Campanile.

'And I need my blinds decorating. I need the painters to recreate the Wolds on my blinds.'

'Scenic artists,' says Sal.

'What?'

'They're scenic artists, not painters. 'Painters' offends them.'

'Precious!' says Izzie. 'Whatever they call themselves they need to decorate my blinds. I need images of the Wolds. Do you know what the Wolds are, David? All that rolling countryside out there. If you want to understand the Wolds, read Hockney.'

'Hockney?' says Campanile. 'Isn't he the pool guy?'

'That was then, David. Keep up. He's done with pool poems. Now he's the Wordsworth of the Wolds. Yes. My blinds need decorating. Images of the Wolds here; the castle here; and over there' - she gestures dismissively - 'Nick's trailer. When the blinds are down I need to see what I would see if the blinds were up.'

11

'They've what?'

'Invited you on set.'

'Give over,' says Oliver. 'What for?'

'They didn't give a reason,' says Jonty. 'Maybe they're fed up of you spying on them.'

'Spying?'

'Peering through windows,' says Jonty.

'Hardly spying.'

'Still.'

Oliver stares at the diamond leading. 'We've both peered through windows, Jonty.'

'Shall I tell them you accept?'

'I don't know,' says Oliver. 'My mind misgives.'

'Eh?'

'Shakespeare,' says Oliver. 'Romeo and - never mind. I've got a bad feeling.'

'About what?'

'Going on set,' says Oliver. 'Some consequence yet hanging in the stars.'

Jonty says, 'Remember when you cracked that mirror at St Peter's? You refused to go out for weeks. But nothing happened. Still hasn't.'

In fact it was Jonty who cracked the mirror, but continued repetition of the lie has made it true in both their minds.

'Not as far as we know,' says Oliver.

'Seven years was up long ago,' says Jonty. 'I think we'd know by now.'

Oliver grunts. He thinks, Perhaps that's why we're still stuck in the East Wing. Perhaps that's why Jaconelli's makes more money out of this place than we do.

Jonty waits.

Oliver says nothing.

Jonty prompts, 'Some people would give a lot to see Izzie Markham up close.'

'Up close?'

'You know what I mean,' says Jonty. 'Watch her working.'

'What people?'

'People,' says Jonty. 'I haven't got a list. It's an observation. Come on, we don't want to miss an opportunity.'

'We?' says Oliver. 'I thought it was me they'd invited?'

Jonty says nothing.

'Alright,' says Oliver. 'Whatever will be, will be. Let he that hath the steerage of my course direct my sail.'

* * *

'I'll watch her place of stand,' says Romeo, 'and, touching hers, make blesséd my rude hand.'

65

Oliver is mesmerised. Mesmerised by the hush. Mesmerised by the intensity. Mesmerised by the process as much as the performance. The crew observing Romeo observing Juliet. Romeo plotting his first move, Sal plotting the progress of his shot.

They're filming in the vast space of the double-height Grand Ballroom - this is the Capulets' feast, after all - but the crew is clustered in one corner, focussed only on Romeo's first glimpse of Juliet. The intensity makes the working space feel small.

A crane extends over the semi-circle of crew. As Romeo speaks, the suspended camera swivels, rises and tilts.

The clipboards are watching the actors, the belt-danglers are watching Sal. All of them are poised, waiting for a signal.

Sal seems unaware of anyone's presence. His monitor is his world. Nothing else exists.

'Did my heart love till now?' continues Romeo.

The camera descends slowly towards Izzie.

Oliver becomes aware of his heartbeat.

'Forswear it, sight!' says Nick. 'For I ne'er saw true beauty till this night.'

True beauty, echoes Oliver, silently.

Jonty's phone pings. Shit. He whirls round and looks accusingly at the 4th AD.

'CUT!' yells Sal. 'Cut, cut, cut! That take is ruined. Ruined! It was perfect and now it's ruined. Who was that? Who? I will not have my movie ruined by half-wits.'

The 4th AD takes half a step away from Jonty and raises both palms.

Jonty realises the game is up. 'Anna Sampson,' he says. He raises his phone apologetically.

66

'Oh,' says Sal. 'You.'

A titanic struggle plays out on Sal's face. Discretion, for once, wins the day. He gestures to the 4th AD to explain.

'No phones on set.'

'I thought it was - '

'Even on silent.'

'Sorry,' says Jonty. 'It's about the tree. Anna says - '

'Silence!' Sal, raises his hand, eyes on his monitor. 'Trees are not important. Go again.'

'Speed!'

'I'll watch her place of stand,' repeats Nick, 'and, touching hers, make blesséd my rude hand.'

Nick contemplates his hand.

The camera rises, swivels and tilts.

Oliver contemplates Nick's hand, then his own. Pudgy, he thinks.

'Did my heart love till now?'

Oliver can't tell whether the line is his own, in his head, or Nick's, for the camera. He's no longer staring at Nick's hand but at Izzie. The camera descends slowly towards her.

'Forswear it, sight! For I ne'er saw true beauty till this night.'

The camera pulls up and back.

The menacing figure of Tybalt steps out of the crowd beyond Romeo.

'This, by his voice, should be a Montague,' says Tybalt. 'Fetch me my rapier, boy.'

Oliver senses scrutiny and looks away from Izzie. On set, Nick Earl is staring at him. Nick's face remains impassive but his eyes exude hostility, as if it was he who had called for a rapier. Impossible to know if the look in

Nick's eyes is a response to Tybalt's presence within the scene or Oliver's outside it. Oliver has seen that look before. Only now does he recognise Nick as the self-important over-bearing pompous oaf who tried to barge his way into the East Wing the previous week.

Nick continues to stare.

Tybalt continues to berate the outsider.

'What,' says Tybalt. 'Dares the slave come hither to sneer and scorn at our solemnity?'

I'm not sneering, thinks Oliver.

'He shall be endured,' instructs Capulet.

Quietly, Sal says, 'Bellissimo. Cut.'

'Cut!' calls the 1st AD.

Immediately the set swarms with crew. Props are re-set, lights are adjusted, mics are checked, faces are powdered.

Just as suddenly the set clears and the scene begins again.

After three more takes of the same few lines there's a break.

Oliver joins the flow of bodies out of the Grand Ballroom, stifling from the heat of lights and bodies and concentration, and into the fresh early May sunshine.

Most of the bodies head for the catering wagons, some to their trailers. Jonty has vanished; Oliver is alone. He glances up at the top window, imagines himself looking down on the scene he's now part of.

He hears his name.

'Lord Mundayne!'

It's the designer, waving him over to the Henry Moore. He can't remember her name. She's tall. Some would say statuesque.

'What is this?' she calls. 'I don't recognise it.' She's talking to another woman who has her back to Oliver.

He hurries over, scrunching gravel. He deviates onto the lawn and the scrunching stops. The designer's elegance makes him conscious of his ungainly gait. And his paunch, accentuated by his waistcoat. He feels himself sweating.

'Henry Moore,' he calls, breathlessly, as he approaches.

'I'm not familiar with it,' says Simone. 'Izzie, have you met Lord Mundayne?'

Izzie turns.

Oliver stops. 'Oh, I...' He extends his hand but he's not close enough. Hand still outstretched, he leans forward. Still not close enough. He takes another step towards Izzie. 'Oliver,' he says.

Izzie laughs. 'So this is what a proper Earl looks like!'

'Actually I'm not... Oh.'

Izzie presents her hand palm down, preventing Oliver from shaking it.

He watches himself take her hand, raise it to his lips. He hears himself say, 'Make blesséd my rude hand.'

The faux motor-drive of a digital camera intrudes.

'What the - ?'

'Unit photographer,' says Izzie. 'You get used to them.'

'So what is this?' asks Simone again. 'I looked it up. It's not catalogued.'

Oliver relinquishes Izzie's hand. '*Large Two Forms (Praying Hands)*. It was a gift to my grandfather.'

'Expensive gift,' says Simone.

Oliver shrugs. 'Uncle Henry gave away a lot of his work.'

'Uncle? Are you...'

'He was my father's godfather. He was a Wessie but he used to come to the East Riding for the sea air. A lot of them did. Still do.'

'Wessie?' asks Simone.

'West Yorkshire,' says Oliver. 'Castleford. Till he went south.'

Izzie says, 'Praying Hands? I can't figure it out. Where are the fingers?'

Oliver remembers clambering on the sculpture as a child and asking the same question. He repeats the explanation he was always given. 'It's abstract.'

'Semi-abstract,' says Simone.

'Looks like it doesn't know whether it wants to be a mushroom or an eggplant,' says Izzie. 'Sorry, "aubergine".'

Oliver is torn between loyalty to Uncle Henry and lust for Moore's denigrator.

'Can't it be both?' asks Simone.

'It should be what it is,' says Izzie. 'Why spend your days pretending to be something else?'

So it's true what they say, thinks Simone. No sense of irony.

Izzie says, 'It looks like it's been left out too long in the rain.'

'I can see it,' says Simone. 'Stand here.'

Izzie takes the opportunity to move closer to Simone.

'Move round,' says Simone. 'It's in the spaces between. In many ways what's not there speaks loudest.'

Izzie backtracks. She says, 'Tomorrow we kiss. This will inspire me.' She makes a show of contemplating the spaces between. She says, 'I see it now. I'll think of it when we film all that stuff about hands and palms and lips.'

'The sonnet!' says Oliver.

Izzie and Simone look at him.

'The first fourteen lines Romeo and Juliet say to each other,' says Oliver, remembering his GCSE. 'They form a sonnet. Then they kiss.'

'Yes!' says Simone. 'True love. So sudden.'

Izzie tries to regain Simone's attention. 'Praying Hands. The perfect inspiration.' She takes one of Simone's hands in both of hers and quotes, 'For saints have hands that pilgrims' hands do touch. And palm to palm is holy palmers' kiss.'

From somewhere outside himself Oliver hears himself say, 'The Kiss! If it's inspiration you're after come to the Library. We've got one of Rodin's maquettes.'

12

'Have you seen this?'

'Do I need to?'

'Someone's got it in for you, Iz. They're planting stories in the press.'

'So what else is new?' Izzie yawns. 'I hate these dawn calls, Flo. Fourteen hours for fourteen lines. It's a bit excessive, even for Sal.'

Flo says, 'Don't you want to know who they've paired you off with this time?'

'Too tired to care. I need more coffee. AJ, be a darling.'

AJ takes Izzie's mug. He makes a show of holding it at arm's length and squinting at the slogan on the side.

Orvane Hall
Shhh... It's Our Secret

He says, 'You visited the gift shop? Without me? Izzie! I'm offended. Wait a second - is the gift shop even open?'

'It was on the step of my trailer.'

'Secret admirer?'

'Usual thing. No note.'

'But you brought it to the make-up trailer,' says AJ.

He puts his left hand on his hip, tilts his head and touches his chin with his right forefinger. 'Hmmm, methinks there's more to this than meets the eye.'

'Coffee, AJ.'

AJ goes to the percolator. 'What kind of slogan is that, anyway? Shit's Our Secret? Seems a bit... counter-intuitive.'

Flo holds up her screen. 'There's a photo.'

'What? Let me see.'

Izzie takes Flo's device. There's an image of Oliver leaning forward, genuflecting, kissing her hand. She brings it closer, tilts it sideways and enlarges her face. 'It's fine,' she says. 'I look fantastic. Beauty too rich for use, for earth too dear.'

'The photo's fine but what about the story?'

'No one cares about gossip.' Izzie is still scrutinising her own features. 'They just look at the pictures. The goss is like the weather. Any way the wind blows.'

'Look at the headline.'

Izzie scrolls up. The headline is a question:

Star Cross'd Lovers?

Izzie laughs. 'In his dreams. He's even older than Nick.'

AJ says, 'Do you think he planted the story? The Earl?'

'I doubt it,' says Izzie. 'He looks like he couldn't plant a tail on a donkey.'

'Why not?' asks Flo.

'I don't know. Too clumsy? Too shy? Too... I don't know.'

'I think he's cute,' says Flo.

'Cute!'

'Cute enough to leave a gift on your doorstep. Who else has access to the gift shop?'

Izzie studies the screen. '*Yorkshire Post*? What's that?'

'Local rag,' says Flo.

'And this columnist,' says Izzie. 'What kind of name is Chichi Boo?'

'A nom de plume,' says AJ. 'At least, I hope it's a nom de plume. Let me see.'

Izzie hands him the screen. 'No one cares about gossip,' she says again.

AJ says, 'People can't get enough of it.'

'OK, they care but they don't *care*,' says Izzie. 'No publicity is bad publicity. Better get started, Flo. You've only got forty minutes left to make me look fourteen.'

Flo raises Izzie's chair with the foot-pump, flicks the cape and lets it settle over Izzie's shoulders.

Florence Luscinia Make-Up - pU-ekaM ainicsuL ecnerolF.

Flo's branding, sublimated into the fabric of the cape, mirrors itself across Izzie's clavicles. An image of a bird sits between the self-reflecting sets of letters.

'New cape,' observes Izzie.

'For backstage interviews,' says Flo. 'I never know whether they're going to shoot you or your reflection.'

'Both,' says Izzie. 'Definitely both.' She watches herself find her best angle.

AJ says, 'Fixated!'

Izzie locks eyes with AJ's in the mirror. 'It's my job, AJ.'

'Not you. The caption. It says, *Fixated: Izzie Markham*.'

'Fixated. I see. Read the rest.'

74

AJ reads, '*Romeo and Juliet... East Yorkshire stately home... Earl of Yoffer-wyke...* blah, blah, blah... Here we go: *Chichi hears that Hollywood starlet Izzie -* '

'Starlet!' says Izzie. 'Star-*Let*!'

'Don't shoot the messenger! Her word, not mine.'

'Nick Parish's word, more like,' says Izzie.

' *- that Hollywood starlet Izzie Markham is fixated on the tweedy Earl-to-be. Some say buff, some say buffoon, but could this be a mismatch made in heaven? Stranger things have happened. Forget Hollywood, forget Bollywood, say hullo to Hullywood*.'

'Hullo to Hullywood?'

'The nearest city is called Hull,' says Flo.

'Hullywood,' says Izzie. 'Right. OK. Quality column.'

AJ continues. 'There's a sub-heading. *'Torn between two Earls.'* Co-star *Nicolas Earl... award ceremony... plastic plant...* blah, blah, blah. Here we are: *And now Ms Markham has been snapped in more seemly circumstances holding court with East Yorkshire aristocracy (above). Sources close to the starlet say that Ms Markham has had a soft spot for Earl-to-be Oliver Mundayne since leaping to his defence at a crew party. 'She's fixated with him,' our insider tells us. 'She won't hear a bad word about him.' So could this be the first photograph of the next Lady Mundayne? As always, Chichi Boo-sters will be the first to know. Chichi has a spy in the camp and her ear to the ground. Watch this space*.'

'Lady Mundayne?' asks Izzie.

Flo says, 'It's what you call a countess.'

'What do countesses have to do with it? He's an earl.'

'An earl's wife is a countess,' says Flo. 'And they're not Mr and Mrs. They're Lord and Lady.'

'You seem to know a lot about it, Flo.'

'I... there's a link in the article. It says if romance blossoms you're in line to become Lady Isabel Mundayne, 13th Countess of Everwick.'

'If romance blossoms? What century does she live in?'

AJ says, 'Isn't it Yoffer-wyke?'

'It's pronounced Everwick,' says Flo. 'According to the link.'

There's a double knock. The door opens a crack but no face appears. 'Ms Markham, ten minutes, please.' The door closes with a quiet click.

Ms, thinks Izzie.

Ms.

She stares into her own eyes. Do I look like a Ms? It's no title for a star. Lady would be more alike in dignity.

Twenty minutes later she arrives on set.

Nick is already there.

On time, for once, thinks Izzie. Is that because he thinks he's got something new in his arsenal?

'Morning Izzie,' smiles Nick. 'Arise, fair sun!'

'Morning Nick.'

Nick turns to Sal. 'What Lady is that - .' He pauses for effect. Background chatter dips. 'What *Lady* is that which doth enrich the hand of... yonder knight?'

Everyone is listening but no one wants to show it.

Izzie fires back, 'A snowy dove that troops with crows, Nick.'

'Oh, Lady Dizzie-bell doth wax lyrical. Have I touched a nerve?'

'More chance of me becoming a Lady than you becoming a real Earl, Nick.'

'Touché!'

'Bambinos, please,' says Sal. 'I will not have my movie ruined by playground arguments. I will not have my movie ruined by niggles about names. What is in a name, anyway? Nothing. Absolutely nothing! Is this an actor I see before me? Isabel Markham? Nicolas Earl? No. Isabel Markham and Nicolas Earl are not here. Isabel Markham and Nicolas Earl no longer exist. Isabel Markham and Nicolas Earl are distant memories. They are insubstantial shadows. So what do I see before me? I see Romeo. I see Juliet. I see tragedy. Begin.'

They begin.

Romeo takes Juliet's hand and adopts a chivalrous pose, genuflecting, her hand half way to his lips.

'If I profane with my unworthiest hand this holy shrine the gentle sin is this...'

Izzie finds herself scanning the semi-circle of crew for Oliver. He was there yesterday. Will he be here today?

'...My lips, two blushing pilgrims, ready stand to smooth that rough touch with a tender kiss.'

'CUT!' yells Sal.

He stands, not taking his eyes off his monitor.

'Chemistry,' he says to the monitor. 'Where is the chemistry?'

He makes a show of looking under the monitor, and behind it.

'There is no chemistry.'

He turns away from the monitor and crosses the set towards Izzie and Nick, gesticulating as he goes.

'My movie needs chemistry. Without chemistry there is nothing. My movie is about all-consuming love. All consuming! It is about giving all for love. It is about disregarding everything but love. It is about the transformative effect of love. The redeeming effect of love. The triumph of love over death! Romeo and Juliet are the world's most famous lovers. Their love is tumultuous. Like a tsunami. They have no control over it. For them, 'nothing else is'. Nothing! They fall in love in fourteen lines and four days later they lie dead in one another's arms. All for love. Their love is written in the stars and their deaths are mapped out by fate. Love consumes them from the moment they meet. From the moment they set eyes on each other. The very moment! But what do you give me? You give me boredom at the baggage carousel. You give me airline passengers waiting for their luggage. Is that my suitcase? No. Is that my suitcase? No. Oh dear, my suitcase is on its way to Istanbul. It will not do! My movie is not about suitcases. My movie is not about baggage carousels. It is not about lost luggage. It is about love. All consuming love. The only thing consuming you two is' - he makes a double-handed philosophical gesture - 'ennui. Ennui! I didn't cast you for ennui. I cast you for chemistry. Chemistry is at the heart of everything. Read Primo Levi. Where is my chemistry? If I wanted ennui I would have cast David Campanile and Anna Sampson. David and Anna. Imagine it.'

Sal takes Izzie's hand.

'If David were to profane with his unworthiest hand this holy shrine, the kiss would never happen. Romeo and Juliet would never fall in love. Anna would still be analysing the fact pattern and David would still be asking interminable questions. He would still be considering the meaning of each word. *Shrine*, he would think. *From* scrinium, *a chest or cabinet for books. An outdated concept*, he would think. *I don't want outdated concepts, Anna*, he would say. *I want something I can hold on to*.'

'*You* are *holding onto something, David*,' Anna would say. '*You're holding onto my hand*.'

'*You know what I mean, Anna. The gentle sin is this.*'

'*"Gentle sin" sends the wrong message, David. How can sin be gentle?*'

'*I don't know, Anna. That's what I hire you for. To advise on these things.*'

'*Well, what do you mean by sin, David? Do you mean an offence or a tort?*'

'*What?*'

'*To sin is biblical, David. We don't live in biblical times. We live in a time of offences and torts - criminal wrongs and civil wrongs. What exactly are you thinking of doing?*'

'*Smoothing that rough touch with a tender kiss, Anna. That's what it says here. Right here, in the script.*'

'*A kiss? That will turn on the question of consent, David. It's a grey area. You know my advice. Do nothing.*'

'Do nothing!' says Sal. 'Always. Do nothing! If Romeo and Juliet do nothing there is no love, there is no death, there is no story. If they do nothing they have no story to tell. Their destinies are unfulfilled.' (Izzie thinks, Maybe they would be happier that way?) 'Doing nothing gets us nowhere. Ennui gets us nowhere. Ennui leaves us going round in circles. Circles! That is why David is the producer and I am the director. It is why Anna is the lawyer and I am the director. I need passion. I need all-consuming love. Enough with the airline passengers. Enough with the jet-lag. Enough with the baggage carousel. Get yourselves through customs and security. Find yourselves and go again.'

Sal returns to his monitor.

79

Nick takes a step closer to Izzie. He leans in and says, 'Something distracting you, Dizzie?'

'Speed!'

'Action!'

Romeo takes Juliet's hand and begins again.

Twelve takes later Sal calls a break. Bodies ebb out of the Grand Ballroom.

Izzie walks in the other direction, away from Nick. She expects to find an alternative exit. Instead she finds herself in the Library gazing at The Kiss.

She's startled by a voice - Oliver asking, 'What do you see?'

She hides her surprise.

'A kiss,' she says, as casually as she can.

'There's no kiss,' says Oliver. 'Not yet.'

'How do you mean?' asks Izzie.

'Their lips aren't touching. The kiss is... imminent.'

She looks closer. 'You're right.'

'They're adulterers,' says Oliver. 'From Dante's Inferno. They end up in the second circle of hell.'

'Nice.'

Izzie is distracted. She's looking over Oliver's shoulder at the diamond-leaded windows. At Nick's pale face peering in behind Oliver's back. She meets Nick's eye, then Oliver's. She reaches a decision. She leans close to Oliver.

'When you say the kiss is imminent,' she breathes. 'What do you mean by "imminent"'?

'A-a-bout to happen,' stammers Oliver.

'Like this?'

They kiss.

13

'She what?'

'You heard, Jonty.'

'I don't think I heard right.'

'You heard,' repeats Oliver.

Jonty nods slowly. 'OK. So. What happens next?'

'Next?'

'Yes. Next.'

'Nothing,' says Oliver.

'Nothing? You don't just kiss Izzie Markham and nothing happens. She's a star. Something happens.'

'Like what?' asks Oliver. 'A wedding?'

Oh my God, thinks Jonty. He says nothing.

'Like what?' repeats Oliver.

'I don't know,' says Jonty. 'Something. You're sure she wasn't trying to provoke someone? You weren't being used? An unwitting agent provocateur?'

'I told you,' says Oliver. 'No one else was there. Just us.'

'Hmmm.'

'I feel...'

Oliver stares out of the window.

'You feel...?'

'Different,' says Oliver.

'Different? Different how?'

'Not the same.'

Jonty waits.

'As if part of me has been missing,' says Oliver. 'All this time. And I didn't know it. And now I know it but it's still missing. I feel incomplete, Jonty. Is that love? To recognise your incompleteness? To acknowledge it? To know where completeness lies? Where does one of us begin and the other end? Who completes whom?'

'A kiss is a kiss, Ol. Not a divine revelation.'

'It was more than a kiss.'

Jonty says, 'She kisses for the camera.'

'There was no camera,' says Oliver. 'Well, there were the security cameras, I suppose. But it was real. I could tell.'

'She's an actress. Her life is a role.'

'You're a lawyer, Jonty, but you're not always lawyering. Sometimes you're you. Occasionally.'

Oliver resumes staring through the window.

Jonty watches him.

Oliver sighs and stands and says, 'I'm going for a walk.'

'OK. You know where I am if you need me.'

What I need is Izzie, thinks Oliver.

He's thinking the same thought as he leaves the room and exits the Hall and crosses the gentle slope of the lawn. He's thinking the same thought when he finds himself walking the curve of the tall orchard wall. High and hard to climb, he thinks, remembering skinned knees and mercurochrome.

He closes his eyes. He trails his hand along the uneven stone. His fingertips register the roughness, the coolness, the changes in texture. Stony limits cannot hold love out. He registers chalk and flint. Grit and sand. Then tongue and groove and flaking paint. He's reached the Orchard Door.

He opens his eyes.

The weathered door is as magical as it always was. An arched door in a high wall? Why not a gate? The Orchard Door was always a portal between worlds and now it is again. He turns the handle. What world awaits?

Now he's standing in what's left of the orchard, palm against an apple trunk, gazing at Izzie's trailer.

His eyes meet eyes at the window.

Not Izzie's eyes.

Whose? thinks Oliver.

The blinds descend in unison, slow and steady.

The setting sun flares off the glass.

When the after-image stops dancing in Oliver's eyes the windows are blank.

* * *

'A kiss?'

'You heard, Flo.'

'I don't think I heard right.'

'You heard,' repeats Izzie.

'Why?' asks Flo.

'Why?'

'Yes. Why? There must have been a reason.'

'I don't know,' says Izzie.

'To spite Nick?'

83

'I don't know,' says Izzie again. 'To shut him up, maybe. Put him in his place.'

'What about the Earl?'

'The Earl?'

'Yes,' says Flo. 'The Earl. Oliver.'

'I don't know,' says Izzie. 'He... it was... not what I expected. He kissed by th' book.'

'What does that mean?'

'It's one of my lines,' says Izzie. 'I say it to Romeo. When we kiss.'

'Oh my God, Izzie. You're not going down that road?'

'What road?'

'Romeo and Juliet.'

'Don't be ridiculous, Flo. It was a kiss, not a divine revelation. Spur of the moment. Meaningless.'

'Meaningless?'

'Yes. Meaningless,' says Izzie. 'But Lady Isabel! Imagine Nick's face.' She shades her eyes from the lowering sun. 'Can you get the blinds.'

'Where's the remote?'

'On there.'

Flo crosses to the rear slide-out and hits the button.

As she stoops to replace the remote her eyes meet Oliver's eyes in the orchard.

The blinds descend.

A vertical wipe.

Oliver is replaced with a replica of the empty orchard and the Wolds beyond.

'What the - ?'

'Not bad, is it?' says Izzie. 'The painters did it.'

'He's - ' begins Flo. Instead she asks, 'Why?'

'Because I wanted it done.'

'Obviously,' says Flo. 'But why?'

'Because Nick's are done.'

'So everything is about Nick?'

'No,' says Izzie. 'This way I get to have my privacy and still enjoy the view. It's not every day you get to gaze at the Wolds.'

Flo says, 'It's not every day you get to have your cake and eat it.'

'What does that even mean? You've got to make the most of these things, Flo. The apple trees. The blossom.'

'But you can't see what's going on,' says Flo. 'You can't see anything.'

'I can see what I want to see.'

'Which is?'

Izzie makes a sweeping gesture. 'This.'

'A backdrop,' says Flo. 'You know your entire life doesn't have to be a role? You're allowed time out. You're allowed to be you. Occasionally.'

'That's not how it works, Flo. The maintenance of stardom. Stars have to shine all the time. Even when no one's looking.'

Whose words are those? thinks Flo. She says, 'What about the people around you? What does it do to them? Pulling down the blinds. Shutting them out.'

'I don't pull down the blinds, Flo. They're electric.'

There's a knock.

Brooke lets himself in. 'Say it ain't so, Izzie. Tell me I heard wrong.'

'Heard what?'

'The Earl.'

'News travels,' says Izzie. 'Who told you?'

'Ellen.'

'For God's sake!' says Izzie. 'It was a kiss, Brooke. What's the big deal?'

85

'Ellen and I are concerned.'

'Concerned? About a kiss? It's not as if I had my way with him over the Library table.'

'Still,' says Brooke.

'It was a private moment. Nick was spying. Peering through the window. I could have him arrested.' She gestures to one of the banquettes. 'Sit. Sundowner?'

Brooke sighs and sits. He examines the bottle. 'Yorkshire gin? What is Yorkshire gin?'

'It's gin made in Yorkshire,' says Izzie. 'AJ visited the distillery.'

'It's infused with tea,' says Flo.

'Tea?'

Izzie says, 'When in Rome.'

Flo knocks hers back. 'I'd better go.'

She goes.

Brooke pours and sips and says, 'So what happened?'

'That's between me and the Earl,' says Izzie.

'Unfortunately it's not that simple,' says Brooke. 'There's a charade to maintain. Audiences need to believe. You know that.'

'Believe what?'

'In the possibility,' says Brooke. 'That there might be something between the leading man and the leading lady.'

'Leading man?' says Izzie. 'Leading lady? What century do you live in?'

'Alright. Between the stars.'

Izzie pours herself another Masons.

'When we arranged for that paparazzo to be in the hotel,' says Brooke, 'behind the plastic plant, your numbers shot up. That stunt took you to the top of the list.'

'What does that have to do with anything?'

'This could go the other way.'

'Are you telling me to stay away from the Earl, Brooke? Warning me off?'

'I'm asking you to be discreet,' says Brooke. He raises his glass to the light, examines it. 'This is good.'

'It was meaningless,' says Izzie. 'What makes you think there's anything to be discreet about?'

'That columnist seems to think she's onto something. The one with the weird name.'

'The *Yorkshire Mail*?' says Izzie. 'That wasn't me.'

'*Yorkshire Post*,' says Brooke.

'Whatever.' She waves away the correction. 'That wasn't me.'

'I know. Ellen has plugged that particular leak. This affects her client too.'

'Affects her client? My God, Brooke, mountains and mole-mounds. It was a kiss, not a marriage proposal.'

'Ellen and I will feed something to the columnist,' says Brooke. 'Just act friendly around Nick.'

'I despise Nick.'

'You're an actress. Be convincing. Be tactile. And be patient with the unit photographer. A picture is worth a thousand words.'

14

'Because a video is worth a thousand pictures,' says Jonty.

'What are you on about, lad?' booms the Earl. 'Don't talk in riddles. Speak plain.'

'The reason the national news sites have picked up the story,' explains Jonty, 'is because of the video.'

'*Our* video,' says the Earl.

'Unfortunately it's not that simple,' says Jonty.

'It never is,' says the Earl. 'Not once lawyers get involved.'

'That's why you've got me,' says Jonty. 'To fight your corner.'

'It's our Library. They're our security cameras. How come it's not our video?'

'It's a grey area.'

'Grey area!' booms the Earl. 'No wonder Dickens said kill all the lawyers.'

'That was Shakespeare,' says Jonty.

'I thought it was Dickens.'

'Shakespeare,' says Jonty.

'I'm surprised you can remember, lad. Never one for details, were you?'

'It was on the whiteboard,' says Jonty. 'First day at law school. Henry the Somethingth. We discussed incitement.'

'Henry Copperfield,' says the Earl. 'I knew it was Dickens. So. What's the plan?'

'Do nothing,' says Jonty.

'Do nothing? Nothing will come of nothing, lad. Speak again.'

'Do nothing,' repeats Jonty. 'It's like the weather. You said so yourself.'

'Blow winds and crack your cheeks? That gave us a right laugh at school. In the days when school was school. Crack your cheeks! Marvellous. Good old Dickens.'

The Earl's laugh becomes a coughing fit.

When he gets his breath back he says, 'Dickens could show these journalists a thing or two about weather reports, eh Jonty?'

'I'm sure he could. He was always one for weather, Dickens.' Jonty congratulates himself on steering the Earl away from the video and onto the weather.

'Any road, enough about the weather. What are we going to do about this video?'

'It's a storm in a teacup,' says Jonty. 'Let it blow over.'

'But they've twisted it, Jonty. They've turned it into something it's not.'

'They've turned it into a story,' says Jonty. 'It's what they do.'

'We need to set the record straight. Get our side across.'

Jonty says, 'Don't feed the monster.'

'Is that your advice? Let them say what they like? Let them get away with it? We didn't win the War by doing nothing, Jonty. By letting Jerry get away with it. We stood up for ourselves. We didn't take any nonsense.'

'You'll be misquoted,' says Jonty.

'They're manipulating the facts. They're making my son look ridiculous.'

Oliver is doing a pretty good job of that himself, thinks Jonty.

'My heir, Jonty. They're making my heir look ridiculous, and that makes me look ridiculous.'

Jonty says, 'Izzie Markham is a star. Facts will always be manipulated.'

'We should do something about it.'

'That would make matters worse,' says Jonty. 'We'd start an arms race.'

'It's already an arms race,' says the Earl. 'That nice picture of Oliver kissing her hand. Then a sneaky shot of her being tactile with that Nicolas Earl. Now this... Library peep show.' He coughs again. 'They've crossed a line.'

'If we leave it everyone will move on,' says Jonty. 'By next week it will be yesterday's news.'

'Tomorrow's chip paper, eh?'

'Yes,' says Jonty. 'Next week it will be tomorrow's chip paper.'

The Earl looks thoughtful.

Jonty hopes that's it. Perhaps the Earl will leave it at that.

'But the video will still be there, Jonty. You can't wrap fish and chips in video.'

'It will be there but no one will be looking at it,' says Jonty.

'Like that tree?' says the Earl. 'In the forest? Nobody hears it fall?'

'Yes,' says Jonty. 'Like that tree.'

He waits. He senses there's more to come.

'What about the law?' says the Earl. 'You're the lawyer. What about copyright? Privacy? All that la-di-dah about data protection. The right to be forgotten.'

'There are defences,' says Jonty. 'Fair dealing, public interest, the journalistic exemption. The right to maintain an archive.'

'Whose side are you on, Jonty?'

'It's my job to analyse both sides of the argument. That's what you pay me for. To be one step ahead. To be prepared for the next move. Like chess.'

'Analyse?' says the Earl. 'Anal, more like. So. How did they get hold of it?'

'Pardon?'

The Earl's question is inevitable but it catches Jonty off guard. He can't remember the response he's rehearsed.

'How did they get hold of it?' repeats the Earl. 'The video.'

'I… I'll talk to the security company,' says Jonty. 'The cameras are monitored remotely. From Leeds.'

'Leeds?' asks the Earl. 'What use is that? It's a good seventy miles.'

'If they see something urgent they contact the police,' says Jonty.

'And if they see something juicy they contact the press. Is that how it works?'

Too good to be true, thinks Jonty. But don't over-sell it. He says, 'I'll have a word with them.'

'And I'll have a word with Hazel's father,' says the Earl.

'Hazel?'

'Hazel Byrne,' says the Earl. 'The gossip woman.'

'The gossip woman is called Chichi Boo,' says Jonty, too loud and too fast. This is a move he was not prepared for.

'Pen name,' says the Earl. 'She's called Hazel Byrne. She was in Oliver's class at primary school, before he went off to St Peter's. Used to come here and climb on the Henry Moore. Those were the days! Oliver wrote her name in his drawing book. Her father was publican at the Eoferwic Arms. He could show these brewery chains a thing or two about running a pub. Hazel and Oliver used to sit on the bar and drink fizzy orange from a pint glass with two straws. The old Eoferwic. Before they turned it into a gastro-pub. It was a proper pub in those days. That's probably where she picked up her taste for gossip.'

'And whisky,' laughs Jonty.

'Eh?'

'Nothing. I heard she likes whisky, that's all.'

'Wouldn't surprise me,' says the Earl. 'It fits. Not very ladylike, is it Olivia?'

Lady Mundayne looks up from her book. 'Sorry?'

'Not very ladylike,' repeats the Earl. 'Whisky.'

'Yes please,' says Lady Mundayne. 'Corryvreckan. With a dash of mineral water.'

The Earl grunts. He asks Jonty, 'What does Oliver make of all this?'

'Oblivious,' says Jonty. 'Can't seem to see what's going on.'

'Plus ça ruddy change,' says the Earl. 'Where is he?'

'Picnic,' says Jonty.

'Picnic? A damned picnic? At a time like this?'

I heard him talking to Anthony about driving him out to the coast,' says Jonty. 'Spurn Head.'

'Anthony Higgins should damn well know better. He drives me, not Oliver. What if I need transport?'

Jonty says nothing.

'Did she go too? Lizzie?'

'Izzie,' says Jonty. 'I assume so.'

'Never assume, Jonty. Didn't they teach you anything at St Peter's? Remind me to ask for your damned fees back.'

15

'This is where I come when I need to be thoroughly alone,' says Oliver. 'I wanted to share it.'

A cold wind cuts through the May sunshine. He's glad of his black coat.

Looking out to sea, he says, 'I thought you'd like it.'

'I do,' says Izzie.

Oliver turns to look at her.

'Like it, that is.'

She's borrowed Oliver's Barbour. She zips it to the neck, and turns up the collar.

'Simply myself,' says Oliver.

The wind whips the words from his lips.

'No one watching. No one listening. No one judging. Just me and the sea and the sky. And you, now.'

Izzie says, 'It's magical.'

'It's a blank slate. It makes me feel sharp-edged. As if I can start again.'

'Why would you want to do that?'

'I wouldn't, necessarily,' says Oliver. 'But the possibility is there. Here.'

'An escape?'

'In a way. Here, I don't have to be anyone. I can be me.'

Izzie says, 'That's what I've spent my life trying to escape from. Being me.'

The brittle spit of shingle extends away from them, pinned between sky and sea. Shrinking into distance, out of reach. A bridge, of sorts, between the edge and what's beyond.

They're side by side, gazing into the indeterminate distance.

Oliver says, 'Can you feel yourself disconnecting?'

Izzie nods. 'Detaching.'

'Disengaging.'

'From the world,' says Izzie. 'Not from you.' She puts her arm through his.

'You can see why they thought the earth was flat,' says Oliver.

'So much sky.'

'All that horizon.'

Izzie says, 'It's a kind of therapy.'

'Outer-edge nostalgia, Ted Hughes called it.'

'What does that mean?'

'What you just said. A kind of therapy. A kind of magic. Philip Larkin called it unfenced existence.'

They cross the shingle to the water's edge and stand and stare at the sea and the spit and the horizon-wide sky.

'Say the name again?'

'Spurn Head,' says Oliver. 'Or Spurn Point. Depends who you ask.'

'I'm asking you.'

'Spurn,' he says.

'Just that?'

'Yes,' he says. 'Just that.'

They retrace their steps and sit. The corners of the picnic blanket are held down by miniature cairns of shingle.

They roll hard-boiled eggs between their palms. The shells craze and crumple.

'What's Eoferwic?' asks Izzie.

'The Earldom.'

'I know,' she says. 'But what is it? What does it mean?'

'Wild boar,' says Oliver.

He peels his egg.

'When the Vikings came they couldn't pronounce Eoferwic so they changed it to Jorvik. And when the Vikings left the English were too lazy to say Jorvik so they shortened it to York. So without Eoferwic, Yorkshire wouldn't be Yorkshire.'

'And the Big Apple wouldn't be the Big Apple.'

'Eh?'

'New York. It wouldn't be New York.'

'I suppose not.'

Oliver carefully puts their eggshells into the tinfoil and crumples it into a ball.

He says, 'I've never been beyond.'

'Beyond what?'

'Yorkshire,' says Oliver. 'No need. We've got everything. Field and fountain, moor and mountain. And this.' He gestures at their surroundings. 'There are more acres in Yorkshire than words in the Bible.'

The wind picks up the balled tinfoil and bounces it over the shingle.

Oliver is up and after it.

As he stoops to retrieve it the wind whips it out of reach.

He renews the pursuit.

This time, he traps it with his foot before bending to pick it up. He returns, breathless.

'My eco-warrior,' laughs Izzie.

'It's important.'

Oliver sits.

Izzie leans towards him.

Deep in Izzie's irises Oliver sees a double image of what's behind him. The finger of shingle pointing nowhere and everywhere.

To the north, in his peripheral vision, there's a glint of reflected sunlight.

'Long lens,' says Izzie.

Her gaze doesn't deviate but Oliver turns towards it.

She puts a gentle finger on his chin and turns his face towards hers.

'Ignore it,' she whispers.

She doesn't tell him she's had Brooke tip off the paparazzo sniper. She doesn't tell him the deal was to make the pictures grainy; furtive. She doesn't tell him this is the nuclear option - the culmination of the arms race.

A moment before their lips meet the distant digital shutter stops time.

Part Two

16

'Now then. What's this?'

'A pre-nup.'

'I can see it's a pre-nup, Jonty. It says "Pre-nuptial Agreement" at the top.'

'Well then.' Jonty sits.

'Were you born in - '

'No need for the door. This won't take long.' Jonty slides the pre-nup across Oliver's desk.

Oliver extends his left hand, places the tips of three fingers against the bottom edge of the pre-nup and slides it back. His little finger and thumb remain aloof. 'What do I want a pre-nup for?'

'You don't.' Jonty extends his right hand, places his palm on the pre-nup and returns it to Oliver's side of the desk. 'Anna Sampson does. She says it's standard practice.'

'Who is Anna Sampson?'

'A lawyer,' says Jonty. 'She acts for Izzie.'

'There's a lot of acting going on.'

'It's what we do.'

'We?'

'Us,' says Jonty. 'Lawyers.'

'Anna Sampson,' says Oliver. 'Is she the Annie Lennox lookalike? Been sniffing around for a couple of weeks?'

'-ish,' says Jonty.

'A couple of weeks-ish?'

'Annie Lennox-ish. Circa 1992, maybe. Not Annie Lennox now.'

Oliver says, 'That poster. Do you remember? In your room at St Peter's.' He murmurs, 'Love, love, love is a dangerous drug.'

'It's savage and it's cruel,' says Jonty. 'And it shines like destruction. Yes. Her. She's a good lawyer.'

'In what way?'

'She's very... thorough. She's been making inquiries. Judging from this' - Jonty pats the pre-nup with the flat of his hand - 'she's decided the estate - the Trust - is a liability. They're only interested in the title.'

Oliver says, 'What does she mean by standard practice?'

'Hollywood stars. She says it's what they all do.'

'All?'

'Everyone. Everyone who's anyone, anyway.'

'Everyone is someone,' says Oliver.

'That wasn't her point.'

'Izzie and I don't need a pre-nup,' says Oliver. 'We're in love.'

'Anna said you'd say that. She said that's what everyone says. Until it goes wrong.'

'We're not everyone,' says Oliver. 'It won't go wrong.'

'Anna said everyone says that, too.'

Oliver says nothing.

Jonty rubs his chin. 'She might have a point, Ol. You've only known each other five minutes.'

'Four weeks and four days, actually.' Oliver looks at the clock. 'And four hours.'

Jonty waits.

Beyond the diamond-leaded windows spring continues.

Oliver says, 'Is it hot in here?'

Jonty shrugs. '-ish. Maybe.'

'Hot-ish? You should have said.' Oliver gestures towards the window. 'Shall I - ?'

'No need,' says Jonty. 'This won't take long.'

'Love isn't about contracts, Jonty.'

'Marriage is a contract.'

Oliver sighs. He leans forward and turns over the cover sheet. 'What does the money clause say?'

'There's no money clause. It's not that sort of contract.'

'You said it's the only clause that counts. First Law of Contracts, you said.'

'It's not that sort of contract,' Jonty says again.

'What sort of contract is it, then?'

'A pre-nup.'

'I can see it's a pre-nup, Jonty. It says "Pre-nuptial Agreement" at the top. We're going round in circles.'

'Are you sure you've thought this through?'

'How can I think it through when you haven't told me what's in it?'

'I don't mean the pre-nup,' says Jonty.

'What does it say? What's mine is hers and what's hers is her own? Isn't that how these things work?'

'No,' says Jonty. 'I mean yes.'

'Which?'

'It's how it usually works but it's not what it says. It's unusual. It's not an ordinary pre-nup.'

Oliver sighs again, leans forward again, looks at the cover sheet again. 'What's unusual about it?'

'It says what's hers is hers and what's yours is your own. Apart from the title. It says whatever happens she keeps the title.'

'She'd keep it anyway,' says Oliver. 'So much for Annie Lennox being thorough.'

'Not if she remarries.'

'For God's sake!' Oliver bangs his fist on the table. 'She hasn't married me yet and you're already marrying her off to someone else.'

'I'm thinking ahead,' says Jonty. 'Looking at the map. Analysing the possibilities.'

'Analysing? Anal, more like.'

'You sound like your father. Yes, analysing. Making sure all your ducks are in a row.' Jonty mimes shooting a row of ducks. 'Planning the route. Putting contingencies in place for bumps in the road.' He thinks of his coccyx, remembers Maidenhead. 'It's what you pay me for.'

'And what are these *possibilities* you've been analysing?'

'If she remarries she'll need permission to keep the title. Unless it's already been agreed.' Once again Jonty pats the document. 'Annie has done her homework.'

Oliver says, 'If she remarries she can call herself what she likes.'

'What if you remarry too?' says Jonty. 'We can't have two Lady Mundaynes.'

'For God's sake,' says Oliver, quietly this time.

'Or should that be Ladies Mundayne?' says Jonty. 'We can't have that.'

'What if I don't sign?'

'You tell me,' says Jonty. 'She's your fiancée. You've known her almost five weeks. You should know.'

'She'll think I don't trust her. She'll think it's built on sand.' Oliver looks at the window, then at Jonty. 'This is a test.' He extends his hand. 'Pass the pen.'

'Are you sure about this?' asks Jonty. The Mont Blanc stays in his pocket. 'If she's setting tests already perhaps she's the one who shouldn't be trusted. In any event, she should know better. The only thing tests test is how good you are at tests. First Law of Tests.'

'Pass the pen.'

'You don't think you should consult the Earl?

'It's not the Earl's decision,' says Oliver. 'He doesn't call the shots any more. Anyway, it's what he wants.'

'What is?'

'This,' says Oliver. 'Marriage. An heir. Tiny feet pitter-pattering all over the estate.'

'Izzie's not - ?' Jonty tries to mime a baby bump but he's too close to the desk. He pushes back his chair and tries again. 'She's not - ?'

'Don't be ridiculous, Jonty. How could she be? We're not married yet.'

'Right,' says Jonty. 'Of course.'

'Talking of which, can you have a word with Tom Martin.'

'About what?'

'The wedding,' says Oliver. 'What else do people talk to vicars about?'

'Tea,' says Jonty.

'Don't talk to him about tea.'

105

'What do you want me to ask him?'

'I don't want you to ask him anything,' says Oliver. 'I want you to tell him which day.'

'Isn't it a bit early for specifics?'

'We haven't got long,' says Oliver. 'Less than a month.'

'You've already named the day?'

'Twenty-first of June,' says Oliver. 'The solstice. At midday. That's when the stars will be aligned.'

'Says who?'

'Flo.'

'It's the longest day,' says Jonty. 'There won't be any stars.'

'Simone says the stars shine all the time, even though we only see them at night. Some of them have already burned out. She says in many ways what we see is a memory.'

'The twenty-first of June,' says Jonty, 'is only twenty-three days off.'

'I know. That's why I need you to talk to Tom Martin.'

'Twenty-three days,' says Jonty.

'It's the first day of summer.'

'It's a bit sudden is what it is,' says Jonty. 'A bit rash. A bit... unadvised. You haven't even signed the pre-nup.'

'Let's get it signed, then.' Oliver extends his hand again. 'Pass the pen.'

Jonty reaches reluctantly into his jacket pocket and proffers the Mont Blanc between finger and thumb.

The nib gleams in the spring sunshine.

Oliver takes it. It's snug in his hand. A good shape, he thinks. Dependable. Trustworthy. He signs.

'Good.'

He hands back the pen.

106

'One more thing. Do you remember our pact?'

'I remember several pacts,' says Jonty.

'Will you be my Mercutio?'

'Mercutio?'

'My sidekick,' says Oliver. 'My best man.'

Jonty says nothing.

'Jonty. Say something. You're making me nervous.'

'Of course,' says Jonty. 'I thought... I didn't think... Of course!'

Formality falls away.

Oliver hurries round the desk to hug his friend.

* * *

'Give her away? What do you mean, give her away? She belongs to Belltower.'

'Not everything is about your studios, David. People have lives.'

'Don't talk in riddles, Anna. What do you mean, people have lives?'

'People have lives, David. Real lives. This is about Izzie's wedding, not Belltower Productions.'

'Izzie's wedding? What wedding?'

Campanile is in the thirty-third floor conference room, alone. He's staring out of the window, his back to Anna's voice.

'Keep up, David. Everybody knows.'

'Everybody knows? I don't know. How do I not know?'

He turns away from the window, paces, returns to the window. He moves his hand towards the glass, fingers outstretched, changes his mind.

'I don't like not knowing, Anna. I want to know.'

'You do know, David. I just told you. And I discussed it with you before. It's why I'm here.'

Campanile resumes pacing. 'You're not here, Anna, you're there. No one is here. I'm alone. The office is empty. Where is there, anyhow? Uptown? Downtown?'

'Yorkshire, England. You know that. I discussed that with you, too.'

Campanile returns to the window. 'You didn't say anything about a wedding. I would have remembered a wedding.'

'David, you've got your back to me. I can hear it in your tone. You're staring out the window.'

Campanile turns away from the window and his suit and his shoes turn with him. He looks at the spidery device in the centre of the conference table. It's poised. Stealthy. Readying itself to crawl away the moment he stops watching. He asks himself, Is this a conference? One person speaking to one other? Two people speaking across an ocean?

Addressing the device, he repeats, 'I would have remembered a wedding.'

'Read the columns.'

'Is that your considered advice, Anna? The gossip columns?'

'It's what our business is based on, David. Some of what they print is true.'

'A stopped clock is right twice a day.'

Anna says, 'Everybody knows.'

'What about a clock with no hands?' says Campanile. 'A clock with no hands could be right all the time and no one would know.'

'And your point is?'

'Print is an outdated concept.'

108

'Everybody knows, David.'

'What about the atomic clock? The atomic clock is more accurate than the sun. Inaccuracies are artificially introduced to keep them in sync. Leap-seconds. The sun's journey across the sky is slowing and the atomic clock is not. But no one sees the atomic clock, Anna. It's locked away in a time-delayed vault. We have to take it on faith.'

'Everybody knows.'

Campanile considers the surfaces of the conference room. Flat planes, hard edges, reflective sheens. The room is set up for groups. All Campanile sees is empty chairs and a blank tabletop. He's alone in a world set up for groups.

He thinks, People have lives.

He says, 'I take it this is a good thing? For the picture. Izzie and Nick taking this step. Making this move.'

'David. Read the columns. You never read the columns.'

'You sound like Sal.'

'I mean it, David. Izzie isn't marrying Nick. She's marrying Oliver Mundayne.'

'Who?'

'The Earl.'

Campanile listens to the distance between them. There should be a hiss, he thinks, or a hum. But there's nothing. No discernible sound. That kind of distance can't be empty, he thinks. He convinces himself there's a quality to the silence. He turns the phrase over again in his head: People have lives.

'David? Are you there?'

'You tell me, Anna.'

'Izzie wants you to give her away. To walk her down the aisle.'

Campanile returns to the window. Give her away. Curious phrase. A relic. Spear and distaff. The patrilineal line. But DNA. Mitochondrial Eve. What would my name be? He can only think back two generations. Brown, Bradley. David Brown, David Bradley.

'David?'

His toecaps and his forehead are against the glass. He says, 'Why me?'

'This is not about you, David. It's about Izzie.'

'It's a genuine question.'

Anna says, 'It's an honour. Her father is... estranged. He won't be invited.'

'I know it's an honour. I'm wondering why Izzie Markham would choose me.'

'It's not like you to wonder, David.'

'It's not like me to play the father of the bride.'

'So you'll do it?'

'Of course,' says Campanile.

As he speaks the words he feels something shift in him.

'I thought... I didn't think... Of course!'

He turns towards the device on the table.

'Just don't make me give her away to Warner Brothers, Anna. Talking of which. Tell me you persuaded Warners to give us Tom Waits.'

17

Tom Waits is standing with his back to the camera, his fingers to the glass.

'The grey-eyed morn smiles on the frowning night.'

The line hangs in the half dark, a guttural growl in the gloom.

More words emerge: 'And fleckled darkness like a drunkard reels - '

(he turns and steps from half dark into half light)

' - from forth the day's path and Titan's fiery wheels.'

His voice is Helios hauling the sun through the heavens behind a flame-wheeled chariot and it's the groan and wheeze of an eighteen-wheeler belching diesel as it grinds through the gears on the New Jersey turnpike.

He begins in darkness, at the window of his cell, fingers to the glass, scanning the eastern clouds.

He turns in a shamanic trance.

When his eyes locate the lens they're looking through it; beyond it.

He's somewhere between a San Diego junkyard and the Orvane outbuilding where he's tending plants as Friar Lawrence.

Somewhere between Stratford and Pomona.

Somewhere.

More words: 'The earth, that's nature's mother, is her tomb - '

(his rheumy eyes narrow and glisten deep in his Naugahyde face. Sal, eyes locked on his monitor, extends an arm behind him and motions the camera closer)

' - What is her burying, grave that is her womb - '

(Images pile up. Drunkards and titans, wombs, tombs, dirt in the ground. Shakespeare or Waits? The lines are blurred. The crew is agog. There's sorcery afoot.)

' - Oh mickle is the powerful grace that lies in herbs, plants, stones... Poison hath residence and medicine power... Full soon the canker death eats up that flower - '

(The earth died screaming. Romeo is bleeding.)

A cheery voice says, 'Good morrow, Father.'

Romeo's greeting is a recalibration. His arrival lets in light, resets the scene on a human scale.

'Benedicite,' replies Friar Lawrence. 'What early tongue so sweet saluteth me?'

* * *

'*pU-ekaM ainicsuL ecnerolF,*' reads Waits aloud. 'Huh. Sounds like a line from a Tom Waits song.' A nasal laugh, 'Henh, henh.'

He's in the chair, under the cape, avoiding his own eye in the mirror. He's refused make-up but the Belltower publicist has sat him here anyway to give the interview a backstage feel.

'Y'know,' says Waits, 'Pythagoras would do that. Write backward. One of his thighs was made of gold. He was a self-harmer.'

No one knows how to respond.

'He'd cut himself and write backward on a mirror with his blood. He'd angle the mirror at the night-time sky. Adjust it so's the words looked like they were written on the yellow moon.'

'Pythagoras did that?' says Chichi Boo. She's sitting behind him, interviewing his reflection.

Waits tips back his head and narrows his eyes, scrutinising Chichi in the mirror. 'I dunno. Did Pythagoras do that?'

Chichi looks at her notebook, hoping to find something there. The answer, or a question, or solace.

Waits says, 'Y'know, Chichibu is a distillery in Japan. I gave up whiskey but I'm big in Japan.'

Chichi writes, 'Big in Japan.' She looks up. 'You're big in Yorkshire, too. What do you make of the Wolds?'

'I dunno. I like your cheese. I like your dry-stone walls. I was a student of dry-stone walling. Right after I finished traffic school. Passed summa cum laude. I like the way you people hold your umbrellas. The way a person holds their umbrella says a lot about them. It's an important attribute. 'Specially when it rains.'

'I hear the production company has taken over the Eoferwic Arms,' says Chichi. 'I was born there. How do you find it?'

'If I could find a book of matches I'd burn it down.'

'Burn it down?'

'Henh, henh. Not really. I have a rule. Never sleep someplace you can't pronounce. Only stay in places named after presidents or wildflowers. Was there a

113

President Yoffer-Wyke? I don't think so. I found a nice trailer park just along the coast. Primrose Valley. No primroses and no valley but plenty of tarmac and trailers. That's what a trailer park needs. Tarmac and trailers. It was founded by a Freemason. I researched it.'

'Let's talk about film,' says Chichi.

'Shoot,' says Waits. 'Henh, henh.'

'You once said you're not an actor, you just do a little acting,' says Chichi. 'Why do you think directors keep casting you?'

'I dunno. I guess I'm like the hair in the gate. I'm an occupational hazard. They think if they invite me in it will stop me sneaking around and getting stuck in the gate. Kind of pre-empting the problem. I'm an insurance policy against myself. It's a superstitious industry. Superstition is rife.'

'Do you like the process?' asks Chichi.

'The first movie I made was five weeks of work for three lines of dialogue.'

'Too long-winded?'

'It was like working up fifty pounds of dough to make one cookie,' says Waits. 'But now I'm in and I'm out. One take Tom, that's what they call me. I'm only here for three days.'

'But you won't have time to visit Whitby! Talking of Whitby, your English accent in Dracula was impeccable.'

'Impeccable,' echoes Waits in an impeccable English accent. In his own voice he says, 'That was when someone told me I should be doing Shakespeare instead of music.'

'And now you are,' says Chichi, lamely. She grips her notebook. 'I have to ask you about the voice.'

'Urine,' barks Waits. 'I drink my own urine. Everyone knows that. But not when I've eaten asparagus. That's a new detail. Write that down.'

Chichi writes it down. She consults her notes again. 'What do you make of Friar Lawrence? Did you ever imagine you'd be playing a man of the cloth?'

'I dunno. Gimme a bullhorn I'll play anyone. I'm from religious stock. All the psychopaths and alcoholics are on my father's side of the family. On my mother's side it's ministers all the way.'

'So you could say you were born to play this role?' asks Chichi hopefully. She senses a headline.

'Lawrence is Franciscan,' says Waits. 'I can do Catholic guilt. Guilt comes natural. One time I spent all my money in a Mexican whorehouse right across the street from a Catholic church. But Lawrence is less friar than apothecary. He's a man who understands plants. He knows how to handle a spade. He can dig potatoes.'

'And that's something you can relate to?'

'I'm always digging potatoes,' says Waits. 'Whenever there's a break in my schedule I dig potatoes.'

'Can I ask about your co-stars?'

'You can ask.'

'What do you think of your co-stars?'

'I'm not a star,' says Waits. 'Or a co-star. I'm not even a twinkle. I'm just a rumour.'

'You've played alongside Sylvester Stallone, Jack Nicholson. Now Nicolas Earl. Earlier I watched you film your first scene with Earl. How was that?'

'He was bleeding,' says Waits. 'But not so as you'd notice. Brave man.'

'Bleeding?' says Chichi. 'Is that a metaphor? Do you mean he's jealous of Izzie Markham and Oliver Mundayne?'

'Never heard of 'em.'

'You must have heard of Izzie Markham,' says Chichi. 'She's a star.'

'Movie-making is very compartmentalised,' says Waits. 'It's a compartmentalised industry.'

'She's playing Juliet,' prompts Chichi.

'I dunno. Most of us have a limited perspective on the rest of us. You know three or four things about somebody and you put 'em together and make a story.'

'Does that happen to you?' asks Chichi. 'People taking a few details and making a story?'

'All the time,' says Waits. 'All the time. You're doing it now. Some English guy asked if he could put me in a novel. Had me speaking with people who don't exist. Gee, we're getting metafictional here. Henh, henh, henh. No one ever asks a fiction writer if he's telling the truth. Did Shakespeare tell the truth?'

There's a double knock. The door opens just wide enough to admit a voice. 'Mr Waits, ten minutes, please.'

'Gotta go marry two young lovers,' says Waits. 'Violent delights.'

'S&M?' asks Chichi, pen poised.

'Life & death,' says Waits. 'Friar Lawrence. Act two, scene six.' His voice drops to a low rumble. 'These violent delights have violent ends and in their triumph die.'

18

'See all, hear all, say nowt.'

'Nowt?'

'Nothing,' says Jonty. 'Say nothing. Zero, zilch, zip.' He mimes zipping his lips. 'It's from a book Oliver gave me.' He nods. 'Yes. See all, hear all, say nowt.'

'What book?' asks Anna. 'Top Tips For Attorneys?'

'You mean lawyers,' says Jonty. 'No. It's called How To Be A Yorkshireman.'

Izzie asks, 'Did he sign?'

Jonty looks at Izzie. She's a star, he thinks. And she's sitting in my office.

He imagines her naked.

The office shrinks.

Jonty says, 'Is it hot in here? Shall I - ?' He mimes opening the window.

'No air con?' says Anna. 'How quaint.'

'I'll let in some air.'

Jonty's office is tucked away at the back of the East Wing. It's the former scullery - a small ground-floor room with diamond-leaded windows commanding a narrow view of the back of the former stable block. He stands, opens one of the windows for a few seconds and closes it again. He returns to his desk.

'Better?'

Anna looks at Izzie. 'What just happened?'

'It's the Earl,' says Jonty. 'He doesn't like random windows open all over the estate. I'll let in some more.'

He repeats the exercise and returns to his desk.

He gazes again at Izzie. Again he thinks, She's a star, and she's naked in my office. Up close. Not many people have that opportunity. He imagines Anna leaving the room. He imagines Izzie, lithe and naked, ascending gracefully onto his desk and reclining there in her nakedness like one of the maquettes from the special collection behind the false bookcase in the Library. It's still hot, despite the extra air. He loosens his tie. He hears his name.

'...distracting you, Jonty?'

'Sorry?'

'Did Oliver sign?' asks Izzie again.

'Yes,' says Jonty, 'he signed.'

Jonty extends his right hand, places his palm on the signed pre-nup and slides it across his desk towards Anna.

Izzie intercepts it. Her fingers brush against Jonty's. She looks him in the eye.

A challenge. Has she read his mind? Is she imagining him naked? He stiffens his sinews, straightens his back.

Anna places the tips of three fingers against the bottom edge of the signed counterpart and slides it across the desk towards Jonty. Her thumb and little finger remain aloof.

Jonty receives the counterpart. He nods acknowledgement and places it carefully in the top

118

drawer of his desk. He takes a key from his pocket and locks the drawer. 'Like the Cold War,' he says. 'A spy swap.'

'Less risk of shots being fired,' says Anna.

Beyond the window shots are fired.

Anna raises an eyebrow.

'Skeet,' says Jonty. He's unsure whether the raised eyebrow is an inquiry or an accusation.

'Skeet,' echoes Anna. Her tone is neutral.

Accusation, thinks Jonty.

He says, 'Clay pigeons. Moving targets. The Earl's favourite.' He closes one eye, extends one arm and mimes shooting a moving target. His ergonomic chair swivels through 110 degrees, twin barrels passing over Izzie's and Anna's heads. He pulls the trigger. The recoil kicks against his shoulder and the chair rolls away from the desk on its castors.

Anna says, 'That must take a lot of practice.'

Jonty grasps the edge of the desk and hauls himself back into place. 'It is practice,' he says. 'For the game season.'

Anna says, 'I imagine sitting ducks are easier.'

'Sitting ducks,' says Jonty, 'are not cricket.'

'It needs to stop.'

Beyond the window more shots are fired.

Anna reaches into the inside pocket of her jacket and extracts her phone.

'Who are you ringing?' asks Jonty.

'You mean calling,' says Anna. 'I'm not.'

'Why the mobile?'

'Cell,' says Anna. 'It's known as being prepared. Thinking ahead. Reading the map. It's what David pays me for. Sal will have an artistic crisis. He'll tell everyone

119

his movie is ruined. *Ruined!* he'll say. *These shots have ruined my shot. This shooting has ruined my shoot. It's a disaster. A tragedy. That take was perfect, and now it's ruined. It can never be recreated. Never! It's gone. Priceless art, lost to posterity. Lost to... gunfire. Gunfire!* That's what Sal will say. Then he will call David. Sal will insist that David does something about it and David will message me. *Anna*, he'll ask, *what does the contract say about gunfire? What does it say about shooting?* And when David messages me' - she waggles her phone slowly from side to side between forefinger and thumb - 'I will tell him I've already dealt with the problem. Because you are about to call Mellors and tell him to cancel the shooting party.'

'I am?'

'Yes,' says Anna. 'You are.'

'Who is Mellors?' asks Jonty.

'The gamekeeper.'

'It's not game,' says Jonty. 'They're clay pigeons.'

'It's a literary joke,' says Anna. 'Call it off.'

'There's nothing in the contract about shooting,' says Jonty. He squints down the barrel, readying himself for another shot, but changes his mind and lowers his imaginary gun. 'I checked.'

Anna sighs. 'Clause 114. Loud and/or Sudden Noises. Specifically sub-clause 114(a), Machinery.'

'A gun isn't a machine,' says Jonty. 'Tractors are machines. Muck spreaders, combine harvesters. Those are machines.'

'A gun is a machine,' says Anna. 'A very efficient killing machine. In any event we will also rely on sub-clause 114(b), Explosions.'

'They're hardly explosions. That clause is for proper explosions. Demolitions. Quarrying.'

'That *sub*-clause covers all explosions,' says Anna. 'To be precise, all explosions within the control or purview of the Licensor, as defined.'

'That's just boilerplate,' says Jonty. 'No one reads boilerplate.'

Anna says, '114(c), Shooting.'

She says, '114(c)(i), Shotguns.'

She says,'114(c)(i)(1) Shotguns (Pest Control).'

She says,'114(c)(i)(2) Shotguns (Sport).'

She says, 'Shall I continue?'

'No,' says Jonty. He's at a loss. He says, 'If you like I can arrange for you to have a go.'

'I'm not a guns person,' says Anna. 'I don't like violence.' She smiles.

Izzie says, 'I'd like to have a go.'

Jonty imagines her naked with a gun. He says, 'A shooting star.'

Anna rolls her eyes.

Izzie smiles.

Jonty reddens.

Anna says, 'If you want to 'have a go,' Izzie, you can do it during the designated times.'

She looks at Jonty and slowly waggles her phone. 'If you'd like to make the call.'

Jonty dials.

While Jonty is talking to the Earl's PA, Anna's phone pings. She looks at it, types, slides it back into the inside pocket of her jacket. 'Good,' she says.

Jonty finishes his call. He asks, 'What attracted you to contract law?'

'Its elegant simplicity,' says Anna.

121

'Offer and acceptance, you mean?' says Jonty. 'Like that rhyme about the Lady and the Knight. She offered her honour, he honoured her offer, and all night long it was honour and offer.'

Anna stares at him.

'Honour and offer,' says Jonty. 'On-her and off-her.' He considers an explanatory mime but thinks better of it.

'That's not a rhyme,' says Anna. 'It's doggerel. No. Simplicity as in precision. Certainty. Everything mapped out. The legally binding nature. The consequences.'

'Like chess,' says Jonty. 'Every move has ramifications.'

'If you say so. Now. I have a plane to catch.' She stands.

Jonty stands too. 'Where are you flying from?'

'Humberside,' says Anna. 'Humberside to Heathrow then Heathrow to LAX.'

'Over the Bridge,' says Jonty. He follows Anna out of the office. 'We're very proud of the Humber Bridge. It's our Golden Gate. Except it's not golden. But then, neither is the Golden Gate. You know, because of the curvature of the earth the towers of the Humber Bridge are - '

' - further apart at the top than the bottom,' says Anna. She's retracing her steps to the Grand Entrance. 'Yes, I know. By an inch and a half. I read the guide book.'

Thorough, thinks Jonty. He lengthens his stride to keep up. Very thorough.

He says, 'I'm going over the Bridge. I've got late night negotiations near Scunthorpe. Can I give you a lift?'

Anna looks blank.

Izzie says, 'He's offering you a ride.'

122

'Oh,' says Anna, still walking. 'No need. I hired a vintage Phelon & Moore. Yorkshire's Harley Davidson, they told me. I want to make the most of my final trip.'

'Classy,' says Jonty. 'There are two P&M's in the Earl's collection.'

'The Earl has a collection of vintage motorcycles?'

'Yes,' says Jonty. 'Finest in Yorkshire. Finest in the country, probably.'

'That's interesting,' says Anna. 'It's not in the inventory.'

Shit, thinks Jonty. He says, 'Is it not?'

'No,' says Anna, 'it is not. That's another of the things that attracted me to contract law. The warranties and indemnities.'

Shit.

'The warranties and indemnities in the pre-nup are very... robust. Ah, here we are. I was beginning to think I'd taken a wrong turn.'

They're in the Grand Entrance Hall.

Anna raises the flap in the cloakroom counter and ushers Izzie through. She turns to Jonty. 'Yes. That's the great thing about contract law. The safety features.' She and Izzie vanish into the cloakroom.

Shit.

Jonty waits for them to reappear. His phone pings.

New message from Anna Sampson: *Full and frank disclosure*. Shit.

His phone pings again: *All material facts*. Shit.

He turns off his phone.

When Izzie and Anna re-emerge Anna is in full bike leathers, helmet dangling from one hand, pannier in the other.

'Right,' she says. 'California, here I come.'

Jonty and Izzie watch her descend the semi-circular steps of the portico. The leathers and bike boots give her a western swagger. She straddles the Phelon and stands, feet apart, knees braced, to fasten her helmet. She leans forward, kicks back and moves away smoothly without disturbing the gravel. Shc takes a perfect line down the shoulder of The Avenue, skimming the outer edges of the speed bumps. At the gate there's a momentary pause and she vanishes in a blue cloud of vintage exhaust.

Jonty turns to Izzie. 'So. Nice to finally meet you face to face.' He extends his hand. 'Till next time.'

Izzie pats her non-existent pockets. She says, 'I seem to have forgotten my copy of the pre-nup.'

'Oh,' says Jonty. 'I can - '

'I must have left it in your office. Silly me.' She turns and walks back inside.

Jonty follows.

They retrace their steps towards the East Wing.

'Nice bike,' says Jonty.

'I don't know anything about bikes,' says Izzie. 'But Anna does. Especially vintage ones. She says not declaring assets is very serious.'

'It's a lawyer thing. We all say that.'

'She says she's got you over a barrel.'

'We all say that, too.'

They continue walking.

'Left here?' asks Izzie.

Jonty nods. 'Actually,' he says, 'I think Anna's missed a trick'.

'Oh yes? What sort of trick?'

'She seems to be working on the premise that the estate - the Trust - is a liability.'

'Trust?' says Izzie. 'I don't know anything about that.'

'It's a lawyer thing. Tax efficiency, it's called.' (In his head a voice sings, *I say efficiency, you say evasion*.) 'Anyway, prima facie she's right - as a whole the Trust has become a liability. But parts of it could be profitable. Once your film is released. Those parts could be hived off.'

'How do you mean?'

'Your fans will come flocking to see where Juliet professed her immortal love. They'll want to stand on the balcony, walk down the aisle, lie in the vault.'

'And?'

'Imagine the merchandise,' says Jonty. 'The coffee mugs and the keyrings and the window stickers. Imagine the marketing opportunities. We could offer star-cross'd weddings. Tie it in with a backstage tour and concessions at the Eoferwic Arms.'

'Star-cross'd is a bad thing,' says Izzie. 'They die at the end. There's a pact.'

'That's exactly what Oliver said.'

'He's right.'

'The point is, Anna has sold you short.'

'And you can do better?' asks Izzie. 'What about Oliver? Isn't that what you lawyers call a conflict of interest? Advising both of us?'

'Here we are.' Jonty opens the door and ushers Izzie into his office. 'You're practically married. What's good for you is good for Ol. There's no conflict. Your interests are aligned.'

'Are you sure?'

'Trust me,' says Jonty. 'I'm a lawyer.'

19

'It's like another world.'

'It is another world.'

Izzie and Oliver are speaking in whispers. The darkness demands it. Yet their voices echo. It's a strange echo. A half-heard sibilance that resonates briefly and ends abruptly, overwhelmed by the vast chancel of the cave.

'Orpheus followed Eurydice into the underworld,' says Oliver. 'Dante found Beatrice there. Here.'

'You didn't follow,' says Izzie. She links her arm through his. 'You led.'

They lean into each other against the damp chill of the underground air.

Oliver has pulled strings. He's had Anthony Higgins arrange with the guides for them to be alone in the Battlefield Cavern, deep in the Craven cave system below Ingleton. They've been guided past underground waterfalls and strange mineral formations - the Witch's Fingers and the Devil's Tongue, the Crown of Thorns and the Sword of Damocles - and squeezed through tunnels and low passageways narrowed by creamy sheets of flowstone. Now the guides have withdrawn and they're alone in wonderland. Around them, spotlights pick out delicate orange stalactites, a static waterfall, stone drapery, a mineral chandelier.

'It's magical,' whispers Izzie.

'All made by water,' murmurs Oliver. 'Water scoured out this cave, then water built these features.'

'How? It's so intricate.'

'Drop by drop,' says Oliver. 'Each drop leaves a miniscule amount of calcite and gradually the calcite builds up into... this.'

'It feels alive.'

'It is alive,' says Oliver. 'It's still evolving. Still growing, drip by drip.'

He steps towards a flowstone pillar rising out of the floor. 'Listen to this.' He taps the pillar and a pure tone fills the cave; a single organ note in an empty cathedral. It's impossible to tell how long the note sustains. Time stretches, or slows, or stops. The tone is there and then it's gone.

'Oh my God,' breathes Izzie. 'I've never heard anything like it.'

Oliver whispers, 'It's the nearest thing on earth to the music of the spheres.'

'It's so... other-wordly.'

'Etherial,' says Oliver.

'Do it again.'

'Best not,' says Oliver. 'I shouldn't have done it at all. First commandment of the cave. They're so fragile.'

'Pretty please?' says Izzie. She puts her palms together.

Oliver glances round, steps forward, taps the pillar again.

Izzie laughs, enthralled.

She says, 'It's like the special effects team took over my mind. Like I'm not real. Like I'm in a movie, playing me.'

'Being down here makes everything strange,' says Oliver. 'It takes you outside yourself. Subverts your senses.'

'How do you mean?'

'We're tuned to open air and sky. Movement all around. Down here it's topsy-turvy. The air is still but the rocks are alive. It defamiliarises things. Your eyes and ears work differently.'

They listen to the sounds of the cave.

'Amazing that a fault can cause something so perfect,' whispers Oliver.

'Whose fault?'

'A geological fault,' says Oliver. 'The Craven Fault. Where grit meets limestone. Strange bedfellows.'

They follow the curve of the steel walkway deeper into the cavern.

'Oh my God!' exclaims Izzie. 'It's me!'

Ahead of them is a face.

'Nature's Mona Lisa,' says Oliver. 'It's why I brought you here. They call this cavern the Louvre of the North.'

'Do they?'

'Not really. But they should.' He leans towards the cave wall and mimics reading a gallery card. 'The Face. Fifteen feet by twenty. Calcite on millstone grit. Number one in a series of one.'

'Check out that smile!' says Izzie. 'Water did this?'

128

'Yes,' says Oliver. 'Nature's tempura. Laid down over millennia, grain by grain. They say twelve monkeys could type the works of Shakespeare. But the rain painted the Mona Lisa first.'

'You brought me to see me!' says Izzie. 'Perfect! The best engagement gift.'

Oliver takes her hand. 'What happens when they finish filming?'

'They edit,' says Izzie.

'I mean for us.'

'Don't worry about that. Brooke will take care of everything.'

'What does Brooke have to do with us?'

'He'll start a bidding war,' says Izzie. 'I'm in demand.'

'I didn't mean work. I meant - '

'The wedding will help,' continues Izzie. 'Weddings are perfect PR. My fans will come flocking to the castle to see where Juliet professed her immortal love and where Izzie Markham became Lady Isabel. Everyone will want a piece of me. Brooke's already started playing the magazines off against each other.'

'Magazines?'

'For the rights,' says Izzie. 'To the wedding.'

'The Earl's not going to like that. Paparazzi trampling all over the estate.'

'It's what everyone does,' says Izzie. 'Everyone who's anyone.'

'Everyone is someone,' says Oliver.

'Very sweet! But somebodies are nobodies. I'm talking about everyone who's anyone, not anyone who's someone. There's a reason more people read magazines than feature in them.'

'Which is?'

'Status,' says Izzie.

The cavern repeats it back to her. Status-s-s-s.

'Ask Brooke,' she says. 'He knows how it works.'

'I don't care about status,' says Oliver. 'I care about us. In two weeks we'll be husband and wife. We'll be able to... be married. I'll see if we can get more rooms.'

'Isn't it your castle?'

'It's complicated,' says Oliver. 'I'll talk to Jonty.'

'What does Jonty have to do with us? Why do you need to talk to him about rooms?'

'He's the family lawyer. He'll know whether we can take back part of the West Wing. So we can have some... privacy.'

'We'll do what I've always done,' says Izzie.

'Which is?'

'Flit.'

'Flit?'

'Between homes,' says Izzie. 'Follow the weather. Any way the wind blows. You need plenty of shoes, though. You don't want to wake up in Santa Monica and find your shoes are in Vancouver. Have you got plenty of shoes?'

20

'By my head, here come the English.'

'Not so loud,' says Ellen. 'They'll hear you.'

'Good,' says Nick. 'I don't care if they hear me. I want them to hear me.'

Nick is slumped over a pint at the bar of the Eoferwic Arms.

'You can be such a pain in the ass when you're in the mood,' says Ellen. 'Why go looking for trouble?'

Nick glares at her.

Ellen sighs. 'Sometimes I feel more like your mother than your agent. Most times, in fact.'

'Pain in the ass how?'

'Belligerent. Argumentative.'

'Argumentative,' mutters Nick. 'Argumentative! I'm not argumentative.'

'And moody. As soon moved to be moody and as soon moody to be moved.'

Nick takes a slurp of his beer. 'Moody moves and movie moods? Is that something you read in Alice in Wonderland?'

'It's a line from your play.'

'Movie,' says Nick.

'Moody,' says Ellen.

'Now who's argumentative?'

Nick has been given a down day. He's spent it perched at the end of the bar, sampling the Wold Top and making frequent trips to the end cubicle of the Gents to polish the lid of the cistern. For the last hour Ellen has been trying to slow him down. She'd been making progress until Jonty arrived with Simone.

'I'll zpeak to them,' says Nick. He giggles. 'I mean speak.' He swivels on his barstool. 'Good evening! A word with one of you.'

Simone says, 'Evening Nick. One word with one of us? Is that all?'

She turns to Jonty and asks, 'Have you met Nick and Ellen?'

Jonty extends his hand. 'Jonty.'

Nick ignores Jonty's hand. 'You're the buffoon's attorney.'

'Nick!' Ellen shakes Jonty's hand. 'Sorry, Jonty, he's been making the most of his day off.'

Nick leans towards Ellen and puts his hand to the side of his mouth. In a mock whisper he says, 'He contort'st with Romeo.'

He turns to Jonty and cups his hands round his mouth. In a mock shout he says, 'Thou contort'st with Romeo.'

'Contort'st?' says Jonty. 'Like at the circus? I don't think so.'

'Contort'st!' Nick giggles to himself and sniffs. 'I mean consort'st. Thou consort'st with Romeo.'

'Come on Nick,' says Ellen. 'Let's go get some coffee.'

132

'Don't worry,' says Jonty. 'It's fine. Can I buy you a drink?'

'One of those,' says Nick. He points at the nearest pump.

'Two pints of Black Sheep, please,' says Jonty. 'And a large pinot noir for my friend. And... Ellen?'

'Masons and tonic, please.'

'Thou art mintels,' says Nick. He laughs again. 'I mean minstrels. You and the buffoon. Two-bit minstrels!'

'Funny,' says Jonty. 'At school Ol and I were in a band called the York Minstrels'.

Simone says, 'Men of many talents.'

Jonty isn't sure if he's being teased.

'What did you play?' asks Simone.

'Fiddle,' says Jonty.

'Really?'

Jonty extends his left hand, adjusts his chin and raises his imaginary fiddlestick. He mimes a jaunty jig.

Simone says, 'I was in a band. A fictional one.'

Jonty lowers his fiddle. 'How does that work?'

'At film school,' says Simone. 'Bulmershe - it's gone now. Subsumed by Reading University.'

'Reading?' says Jonty. 'Isn't that near Maidenhead?'

'-ish,' says Simone. 'Near-ish. Anyway, the band was called The Sticky Sisters. Our only gig was in the background of a backstage scene. All smoke and silhouettes.'

'Very Wim Wenders,' says Ellen.

Nick grunts.

'The camera was backstage, looking over the shoulder of the protagonist at the crowd in the auditorium watching the band on stage,' says Simone. 'Looking through the performance. All you could see was our backs

133

and the sweaty faces in the mosh pit beyond. In many ways the viewer was looking herself in the eye. We - the band, The Sticky Sisters - were a vehicle for the metafictional conceit. One audience looking into the eyes of another. But not vice versa. One audience was looking into a mirror, the other was looking into a void. I was on sax.'

'Tricky instrument,' says Jonty.

'Fictional sax is easier than the real thing,' says Simone. 'It's like faking anything. People believe what they want to believe. You just have to give them enough space.'

'What did Oliver play?' asks Ellen.

'Oliver?'

'In your band. At school.'

'Oh,' says Jonty. 'Bass. He would channel John Deacon. He even had the tank top.'

'He's a villain!' says Nick. 'A base villain.'

'What?' says Jonty. 'Oh. Yes. Very good. A bass villain!' He mimes playing bass.

The drinks appear on the bar.

'Anyway,' says Jonty, taking advantage of the distraction, 'we'll leave you in peace. I came for Simone's aesthetic advice. Make sure my wedding present is tasteful.'

Nick snatches up his pint and some slops over the side. He snarls, 'Wedding! It's a sham. You keep Romeo away from Izzie.'

Ellen looks round to check no outsiders are listening. She doesn't want this on yorkshirepost.co.uk.

'Sorry Nick,' says Jonty. 'I'm his lawyer, not his keeper. Who he marries is his business.'

'Marries!' snarls Nick. He takes a gulp of his pint. 'It's a sham. Anyone can see that. She's not interested in him. All she's interested in is getting one up on me. My name is Earl so she wants to call herself a Countess. The only thing she's interested in is his title.'

Ellen hisses, 'Keep your voice down, Nick!'

'I'm his lawyer, not his keeper,' says Jonty again.

He takes his pint, sips some to avoid it slopping over then raises it to Ellen and Nick. 'Cheers.'

He turns away and ushers Simone towards an empty table.

Ellen sighs. 'Can't you and Izzie call a truce? Or at least make it *look* as if you've called a truce? This wedding will be good for the movie. And if it's good for the movie it's good for you.'

And, she thinks, if it's good for you it's good for me.

'Just give them your blessing, Nick. Even if you have to act, for once. Can you still manage that?'

'A plague on both their houses,' says Nick. 'They deserve each other.'

Ellen puts a hand on his forearm.

Nick's instinct is to shake off Ellen's hand but he finds he's lost interest in arguing. He stares into his pint. He mutters the words again. 'A plague on both their houses.'

21

'So smile the heavens upon this holy act,' intones the Reverend Martin. He scans his celebrity congregation.

St Hilda's is the fullest he's seen it since Songs of Praise. Fourteen years between full houses, he thinks. Fourteen years of failing box office.

Now, as then, he disapproves of the worldly presence of the cameras and the lights and the sound equipment. Now, as then, his disapproval doesn't extend to the wearing of make-up for the occasion.

Earlier, he sat in Flo's chair and read her name forwards and backwards in the mirror, like an incantation. He submitted himself to Flo's ministrations and while she attended to the surface he attended to the substance. He looked into himself in Flo's mirror and he considered those fourteen barren years and he questioned his purpose; his calling. There must be more to life, he thought, than christenings, weddings, funerals, and "More tea, vicar?" Or is it true? We give birth astride a grave and everything between is tea leaves and coffee spoons? Yes, he sat in Flo's chair and he stared deep into his own eyes and what he saw was his own eyes staring deeply back at him.

Flo's make-up is more sophisticated than the BBC's was fourteen years ago. Never before has the Reverend Martin had his eyebrows threaded. Not even when Look North came to interview him for a segment on whether St Hilda was in fact Hild or Hilda and whether she really did turn a plague of snakes into the ammonites found along his parish's part of the North Yorkshire coast. For weeks afterwards he'd overheard people referring to him as the Fossil.

The Rev's words are still hanging in the air. 'So smile the heavens upon this holy act.' He scans his celebrity congregation and he waits. The chatter diminishes. Heads turn towards him. A face from Dynasty meets his eye, more familiar than any of his usual smattering of congregants, and he has to restrain himself from nodding a silent greeting.

The congregation is hemmed in by the Mundayne dead. With their elaborate memorial stones and intricate alabaster effigies the Mundaynes have made the church a private mausoleum. For centuries, services at St Hilda's have been as much about the remembrance of Mundaynes past as the worship of the Almighty. It's something the parish priests of Eoferwic have had to accept, like their colleagues in the churches of Harewood, Barnburgh, Sheriff Hutton and Methley. Generations of Yorkshire gentry have used their churches to cement the association of lineage with location. The phenomenon is replicated across the Ridings in an avalanche of alabaster. Many of the late Mundaynes watching over the ceremony are clad in alabaster armour, their oversized alabaster hands folded over their alabaster chests, their chipped alabaster eyes staring sightlessly from the past into the future, all of them asking the question, What will survive of us?

The Rev waits for silence. He raises his palms in an ambiguous gesture. Is he asserting authority or beseeching validation? Are the congregants in his hands or is he in theirs?

'So smile the heavens upon this holy act,' he says again, 'That after hours with sorrow chide us not.'

He smiles.

He's pleased with his unconventional opening couplet. It complements his unconventional eyebrows.

Amen, amen, thinks Oliver at the altar. But why talk of sorrow? No sorrow can outweigh the joy of one moment with Izzie. He glances to his right. Jonty is at his side. His best man. He resists the temptation to turn and see if his bride has entered the nave.

'We are gathered here today…' intones the Rev. He's exhausted his unconventionality. He runs a finger along his eyebrow in subconscious compensation.

Oliver hears the rhythm of the Rev's voice but not his words. He hears the swell of the organ as Izzie makes her grand entrance. Here comes the bride, he hums, all dressed in white. The Bridal Chorus - despite Sal's attempted directorial input. Sal had voiced his objection to Wagner and Izzie had voiced her insistence. Brooke had reminded Sal who had invited whom to whose wedding and Wagner had prevailed.

All eyes are on Izzie as she makes her stately progress down the aisle. All eyes except Oliver's - he doesn't want to tempt fate by turning too soon. He senses her veiled presence drawing closer. She appears in his peripheral vision. At last she's facing him, across the

138

aisle, on the arm of David Campanile. Her gown and veil are red.

The ceremony progresses.

The Rev intones, 'If anyone here present. Knows of any reason.'

Bodies shift in pews as thoughts are suppressed - humour at the notion of objections, a frisson of what ifs. Ellen glances at Nick, Nick glances at the door of the church.

The sun hits the stained glass window and unconventionality descends once more upon the Rev. 'Knows of any reason,' he says, 'why these star-cross'd lovers may not lawfully.'

Sal raises his palms to his cheeks, jaw ajar in a silent scream. First Wagner, now this.

'The vows you are about to make,' continues the Rev, looking at one then the other.

'Do you?'

'I do.'

'Do you?'

'I do.'

Flo is at the lectern. 'From the Song of Songs,' she announces, 'which is the Song of Solomon.' She looks at Izzie, then at the congregation. 'Let him kiss me with the kisses of his mouth.' Her voice wavers. She looks at Oliver. 'For your love is better than wine.' Another waver. The congregation wills her on. She pauses, breathes deeply. 'As an apple tree among the trees of the forest,' she continues, 'so is my beloved.' Her voice settles. The congregation relaxes. 'Behold, there he stands behind our wall, gazing through the windows, looking through the lattice.' She remembers the vertical wipe of Izzie's blinds. She reads on. She concludes, 'My beloved speaks, and says to me, "Arise, my love, my beautiful one, and come away, for behold, the winter is past.'"

Here endeth the Lesson.

The Earl smiles. He looks proudly at the Countess. Things are going swimmingly.

The Address, unusually, is shared. The Rev introduces the theme: marriage as a voyage into the unknown. He introduces his American counterpart, Josh Rogan. 'Father Rogan and I,' he says.

A strangled sound struggles in the Earl's throat. A proto-cough or gargle that evolves into a growl and threatens to erupt. His body begins to quake and his face begins to colour. His fingers clench and unclench, clutching and releasing some invisible object. Beyond the stained glass a cloud covers the sun and the light in the church dims. The Countess lays a gentle hand on the Earl's forearm to forestall the booming question that's fighting to escape: '*Father* Rogan? She's not a - ?'

'Later,' whispers the Countess. 'Think of your blood pressure.'

The Rev, oblivious, continues to intone. He's warming to his theme. 'Have the faith of a saint in a coracle,' he says. 'Sail together over the spirited waves! Be one another's anchor. Be one another's safe haven. Be each other's guiding light! God has given us the tools to do these things for one another, to be these things for one another. To be one another's lodestar. The sky is anchored on Polaris, the North Star. The North Star locates us. It reminds us where we are, who we are, in the scheme of things. It puts us in our place. It's the key to the map. So we ask ourselves, how do we find our North Star? Well,' says the Rev, 'God has made that easy for us. God put the North Star in the north.'

140

Father Rogan takes up the baton. 'When the Deacon reads from the Gospel,' he says, 'he does it on the north side of the church. Ideally he does it with his back to the congregation, facing the north wall.'

Rogan turns his back to the congregation and faces the north wall.

'And,' says Rogan, 'the reason the Deacon does this - '

(He's forced to stop, overcome by the screech of his radio mic. Turning his back has forced the sound engineer to crank up the gain. He waits for the screech to diminish to an intermittent whimper.)

' - And the reason the Deacon does this,' repeats Rogan, still facing the wall, 'is because the north is untamed. The north has not yet heard the Gospel. Or the north has heard but not listened. The north is the dark region. The infernal region. That is the reason certain classes of people are buried on the north side of the churchyard,' he says, his back to the congregation, gesticulating at the wall, arms high and wide, voice rising, mic squealing. 'Suicides! The unbaptised!! The not-very-respectable!!!'

The Rev cuts in. 'And yet according to the psalms God resides in the Far North. So we ask ourselves. Where is the north?'

The Rev pauses, giving space to his rhetorical question.

Rogan turns.

Quickly the Rev answers his own question before Rogan can answer it for him. 'From where we stand,' says the Rev, 'the north begins just south of where we... stand. And it ends to the north. But if we stand south of where we stand the north begins to the north and ends even further north. In other words - in layman's terms - the

141

north is a movable feast. Like Easter,' he clarifies. 'But without eggs.'

'The north is a concept,' says Rogan.

'A state of mind,' says the Rev.

'A state of being,' says Rogan. 'A way of life'.

'The north is a struggle between dream and reality,' says the Rev. He smiles, surprised at his own words. He's pleased at the unexpected direction in which they're leading him. But what do they mean? No matter, he thinks. Words continue to pour forth. 'North is everywhere and nowhere,' he says, 'everything and nothing. North is nought degrees nought, zero degrees zero. Alpha and omega, the beginning and the end. And so,' he says,' sensing that his journey is in danger of extending itself too far into uncharted territory, 'we end where we began, just as in life. All journeys are circular. Our message, Father Rogan's and mine, as the happy couple embark on their journey into the unknown, is this: Bon Voyage!'

Next, for reasons known only to Izzie, there's a choral rendition of Blowin' in the Wind.

Then the vows.

The Rev has consented to the star-cross'd lovers sprinkling the liturgy with lines from Shakespeare. Izzie takes Oliver's right hand in hers. 'My bounty is as boundless as the sea,' she says, 'My love as deep. The more I give to thee the more I have, for both are infinite.' (But the sea isn't infinite, thinks Oliver. It ends at the shore.) Izzie releases his hand. Oliver takes hers and addresses the Rev. 'Do thou but close our hands with holy words,' he says, 'then love-devouring death do what he dare.'

The Rev closes their hands.

142

Jonty presents the rings.

'A symbol of unending love and faithfulness,' intones the Rev. 'Incorporate two in one. I now pronounce you.You may now.'

Izzie raises her veil.

Oliver leans forward.

Shutters click.

A fraction of a second before their lips meet there's a shout from the back, 'Hold that!'

They freeze. Their kiss remains imminent.

'Thank you. Go again, please.'

Izzie lowers her veil. The Rev repeats, 'You may now.' The veil is raised again.

'Those whom God has joined together,' says the Rev, 'let no man - '

Jonty drops the ring box. Shit. 'Sorry, sorry.'

' - put asunder.'

'Now for the binding bit,' says Jonty.

The signing of the register takes place before the congregation. It's part of the performance, mapped out by the movement director, backed by an organ voluntary.

An opulent T of deep pile red carpet is rolled out before the altar. AJ and Brooke appear with the Beckhams' golden chairs and place them reverently on the plush carpet. They withdraw, stepping backwards in time to the music. They return with an ornately scrolled escritoire, sourced by Simone to complement the Beckhams' burnished thrones. The Beckhams are absent, in Antigua, but they have signed a certificate of authenticity assuring Izzie these are the very chairs.

The bride and groom seat themselves.

The Rev places the register before them on the escritoire, open at a blank page.

143

Jonty presents a box tied with a bow. Izzie pulls one of the loose strands of the bow. Oliver pulls the other. Jonty lifts the lid. A Pininfarina inkless pen.

Inkless? mouths Oliver.

'Ethergraf nib,' says Jonty in an undertone.

'What? How does it write?'

'The nib,' says Jonty, 'is made from ethergraf.' He mimes writing. 'It oxidises the paper. Makes a permanent mark. Let's get this contract signed.'

Oliver watches his name appear before him, burning itself indelibly into the parish register: Oliver Marmaduke Mundayne. A branding of sorts. He considers the process that transmits the letters of his name from his head to the hand that holds the pen; the wiring and the machinery and the interface that deliver his identity from synapse to page. He watches Izzie's name materialise beside his own: Isabel Salome Markham.

22

'What if someone comes in?'

'Someone?' Jonty's voice is muffled.

'Anyone.'

'No one will,' says Jonty, still muffled. 'Everyone's at a wedding, remember.'

'My we - e - edding!' Izzie's voice rises and wavers as Jonty's tongue tips velvet beneath the layered lace skirts of her wedding dress.

She's sitting on the edge of Jonty's desk. She leans back, sweeping her arm behind her, knocking over the inkstand. Her thighs clamp Jonty's head.

He can't breathe.

He thinks, What a way to go.

Stars cross his field of vision.

He stills his tongue and the pressure eases.

'Anyway,' he says, 'they can't. Come in, that is. I locked the door.'

Still kneeling beneath Izzie's skirts, he extracts the key from the waistcoat pocket of his morning suit and holds it up behind his bent back as evidence.

Izzie asks, 'Is that a trick you learned in law school?'

'It's called thinking ahead,' says Jonty, still muffled. 'Being prepared.'

'What about the window?'

The window!

Jonty emerges from under the wedding dress.

Izzie twists at the waist to check behind her. In accordance with the Earl's instructions the diamond-leaded window is closed, despite the heat.

Jonty says, 'There's no one there.'

'What if someone comes?'

Jonty waggles his tongue at her.

'Appears,' says Izzie. 'At the window.'

'No one will appear at the window,' says Jonty. 'Everyone's - '

Izzie pushes his head down. Oliver has appeared at the window.

Jonty's muffled voice says, 'Here's a trick I learned in- '

'Quiet!' hisses Izzie.

She clamps her thighs to prevent Jonty re-emerging. She watches Oliver use the diamond-leaded panes as a mirror to straighten his hair. She watches him lean back to check his look, lean in again, closer, and stick his finger in his eye.

Outside, as Oliver leans in close to adjust his contact lens, his shadow obscures his reflection and he sees Izzie's face where his own had been.

She waves.

Oliver waves back. He starts to perform a complicated charade.

Izzie shrugs and shakes her head.

146

Oliver gives up the charade and mouths, 'They're wondering where we are.'

Izzie mouths, 'I can't hear you.'

Out loud Oliver says, 'They're wondering where we are.'

Every word can be clearly heard through the ill-fitting diamond-leaded panes.

Jonty's muffled voice says, 'Who's that? Sounds like Ol.'

Izzie squeezes harder to keep him quiet.

Jonty's head spins and he's back on the playing fields of St Peter's, trapped in the scrum.

'They're wondering where we are,' Oliver says again, louder.

Izzie says, 'I lost my way.'

'Don't worry,' says Oliver. He draws a half circle in the air. 'I'll come round.' He uses two fingers to indicate walking. Then he reiterates the half circle to represent the journey from Jonty's office window to the front of the Hall. 'Stay there! I'll come round.'

23

'Fiddlesticks!' booms the Earl. He extracts a fob watch from the waistcoat pocket of his morning suit. 'Where the Dickens are they?'

'Don't swear Marmaduke,' says the Countess. 'You'll set yourself off coughing. You know very well where they are. They're taking photographs. For that magazine.'

'Photographs!' booms the Earl. 'It doesn't take this long to snap a few photographs. I could show them a thing or two about taking photographs. Point and shoot, that's all it is. Point and shoot. They need to get out on the skeet range. Get some proper practice in.'

The Earl and Countess are standing at the entrance to the Long Gallery waiting to welcome the guests.

The guests are pressed into the Lilac Ante-room waiting to be welcomed.

Everyone, while they wait to welcome or be welcomed, is consuming champagne and canapes. The rate of consumption and the volume of chatter increase in direct proportion to the waiting time.

Campanile is at the window of the crowded ante-room, fingers against the glass, gazing into the middle distance. He's mesmerised by the Mundayne boar on the church tower. By the intermittent glints as the boar turns in the breeze, catching the sun. He considers the nature of light. Wave or particle? Let's call it radiation, he thinks. Electromagnetic radiation in the visible spectrum. He considers the interplay of solar radiation and earthly forces on the tinplate boar. Dots and dashes of light. Is it a signal? Is someone signalling him? A higher being? He tries to decode the message.

'David?'

Anna is waiting for an answer to her question.

'David!'

He turns.

'Give her away, Anna. That's what you said. Walk her down the aisle, you said. I've walked her down the aisle and I've given her away. You didn't say anything about a line-up. You didn't say anything about greeting guests. That wasn't part of the deal.'

'You're the father of the bride, David. The line-up is part and parcel of giving her away. It's your role.'

'You didn't say anything about a line-up. I would have remembered a line-up.'

'It's in the small print, David. You never read the small print.'

'That's what I pay you for, to read the small print. Do I need to find another attorney, Anna? I can always find another attorney.'

'It's just a line-up.'

'Just a line-up? If it's just a line-up you can line up with me.'

'Fine, David. If that's what it takes I'll line up with you.'

She ushers him round the perimeter of the room, skirting the noisy crowd of waiting guests, towards the Earl and Countess.

The Earl spots them. He booms, 'You must be Markham.'

'No,' says Campanile, 'I - '

'It's a relief, eh, Markham? Getting shot. Clearing the nest. I've been on your side of the fence. Two daughters. Always thought they'd marry Jonty but they never did. And this must be your good lady wife.' The Earl extends his hand.

'No,' says Anna, shaking his hand. 'I - '

'You must be relieved too. Don't know why we need all this hanging around, though. Photographs! We didn't have photographs in our day. No hanging around on the big day. All the hanging around was done in advance. We sat for an oil painting, Olivia and me. Took three weeks.'

'We had photographs as well, Marmaduke.'

'Well we didn't hang around,' says the Earl. 'Not on the big day. They got on with things in our day. The photographers took a back seat. So, Markham, how's your speech coming on?'

'My speech,' says Campanile. He extracts his phone from his pocket. 'Excuse me just a moment.'

'My speeches were marvellous,' says the Earl. 'Both times. Unaccustomed as I am to public speaking, not so much losing a daughter as gaining a son, all that. They loved it.'

Anna's phone pings. New message from David Campanile: *You didn't say anything about a speech.*

The Earl continues, 'What you need to make it interesting is a good prop, Markham. Something visual to hold their attention. Something to build up to. I had a marvellous prop. Marvellous.'

Campanile's phone pings. New message from Anna Sampson: *Part and parcel.*

'Their baby teeth,' continues the Earl. 'That was my prop, Markham. Kept them in a snuff box all those years.'

I would have remembered a speech.

'Handed them to the groom at the end of my speech. Wanted to make sure he had the whole package. Didn't want to be accused of holding anything back.'

Small print.

'Not sure I gave the right teeth to the right groom, though.'

The Countess says, 'I didn't catch your name, dear.'

'Anna,' says Anna. 'This is David Campanile, the producer.'

'Producer!' booms the Earl. 'That's one way of putting it, eh Markham? Producer! So, Hannah, what was Lizzie like when she was growing up? Looks like she must have been a handful.'

'In her teens,' says Anna, 'she was a biker.'

'Motorbikes?' says the Earl. He looks at Campanile. 'Markham doesn't look the type.'

Anna says, 'She got it from me.'

'From you?' says the Earl. 'Well. Nothing wrong with that. Been going on since the ancient Greeks. I could show you a thing or two about motorbikes. You must see my collection while you're here. Olivia, don't let me forget to show Hannah the bikes while she's here.'

Anna says, 'I'd love to.' She smiles.

151

'My pleasure,' booms the Earl. 'My pleasure. Where's Keltbray? Book it in with Keltbray, my aide-de-camp. Get him to put it in the diary. I'll give you the full tour. There are some real gems. I've got a P & M Panther. Maybe two. They knew how to build bikes in Cleckheaton.'

'I'd love to,' Anna says again.

'There are some of your Yank bikes, too,' says the Earl. 'You'll like those. Army issue. You left them here after the War. Harley-Davidsons.'

'WLAs?' asks Anna.

'That's the one,' says the Earl. 'That's the one. WLA. Beautiful noise they made, those bikes. Takes me back. I used to pedal round the Estate in my buckled shoes and short trousers pretending I was on one of those. Twisting the handlebar grips, making that noise. Those were the days. Ah! At last. Here comes the bride.'

'And groom,' says Campanile.

The Countess says, 'Izzie you look beautiful. Look at your face, you're positively glowing. Marriage suits you!' Quietly she confides, 'All I remember about my wedding day is being nervous.'

'Nervous!' booms the Earl. 'Whatever for, Olivia?'

'I remember it like it was yesterday,' says the Countess. 'I smoked a whole packet of cigarettes. I've never smoked before or since.'

'Found her in the bridal suite blowing smoke up the chimney,' says the Earl. 'So, Oliver, what have you kept us hanging around for? It had better have been important.'

'Jonty had some negotiating to do,' says Oliver.

'Sorry about that,' says Jonty. 'Can't rush these things. Now, shall we - '

'Negotiating?' says Anna.

152

'Yes,' says Jonty. 'Tying up loose ends. With the magazine. Shall we - '

'Magazine?' says Anna. She stares at him. Note to self, she thinks. Talk to Brooke about loyalty.

Jonty looks away. 'It's a big deal, he says. Half a million. These things take time.'

'Well now you're here, let's get on with it,' says the Earl. 'Are we supposed to stand in some sort of order? Just like the CCF, eh Jonty? Privates on parade.'

'Privates on parade is something different,' says Jonty. 'Where's Flo? We can't have a line-up without the maid of honour.'

Flo is located and the floodgates are opened. The guests mass up against the bottleneck. Hands are shaken and greetings are exchanged. Names are instantly forgotten. Guests emerge into the Long Gallery, regroup, make their way to their tables. The bottleneck clears. The bride and groom are seated.

The Rev rises, bangs a spoon for grace. 'For what we are about to receive,' he begins. Then he remembers his eyebrows and the wedding at Cana and changes tack. 'Bless us, O Lord Divine,' he says, 'who changed the water into wine; have mercy on we foolish men, who try to change it back again.'

Bread and fishes appear miraculously on the tables: loaves from the local artisan bakery, seafood from Scarborough, Bridlington and Filey.

Two glazed Mundayne boars are wheeled in on spits and carved at the tables, their mournful eyes staring sightlessly at the diners.

White wine turns to red, red wine turns to brandy.

Howard Keltbray tings a teaspoon against a glass. He announces, 'The Father of the Bride.'

The Earl claps his hands and booms, 'Bravo Markham.'

Campanile stands. 'Two households,' he begins, 'both alike in dignity.'

Anna rolls her eyes.

Sal crosses himself.

Campanile wants to impose himself by pacing the length of the table, back and forth, pausing occasionally for effect, but he's trapped.

He wants to assert himself by staring out of the window as he speaks, his back to his audience, but he's on the windowless side of the Long Gallery.

He wants to press his fingers against the diamond-leaded panes and think of elsewhere. More than that. He wants to be elsewhere. He wants to be in a different part of the galaxy, or alone in a featureless room.

'In fair Orvane where we lay our scene,' he continues.

Keltbray tings again. The Groom.

'From the moment I set eyes... Henry Moore... Library, The Kiss, gossip column... pedestal... Spurn… gossip column, Battlefield Cavern.'

'So really,' concludes Oliver, 'it's all thanks to Rodin and the *Yorkshire Post*.'

Ting. The Best Man.

24

'Why didn't you say anything?'

Jonty says nothing.

Which is worse, he thinks. To say he didn't know or to say he knew and didn't say?

He swirls his brandy. He says, 'I don't know.'

'You don't know.' The Earl's voice is ominously quiet. 'It's your job to know, Jonty. It's what I pay you for.'

'I thought you knew,' says Jonty.

'You know me well enough to know I didn't know. You know if I'd known I wouldn't have let this happen.'

'It was an unknown unknown,' says Jonty.

'Don't talk in riddles, lad. You should have known.'

'I didn't know I didn't know. If I'd known there was something I didn't know I'd have known there was something I needed to know.'

'It's your job to know what you know and what you don't know.'

'I know,' says Jonty.

The Earl's study feels like the headmaster's office at St Peter's.

155

The sound of revelry drifts down from the Long Gallery.

'What do you think, Olivia?'

'She's a lovely girl,' says the Countess. 'Did you see her face? She was positively glowing. Marriage suits her.'

'She's a flipping Catholic! I don't want my heirs riddled with guilt.'

'Glowing!'

'And I don't want my estate being snaffled by Romans and frittered away on idols.' The Earl coughs, waits, coughs again. 'The monasteries were dissolved for a reason, you know.'

Your ancestors rose up against that, thinks Jonty. One of them ended up with his head on a spike on Micklegate for his troubles.

'Jonty, what does the Trust say about Catholics?'

'I'll need to look at the deed.'

'What do you need to look at the deed for? You must know it inside out and back to front by now. Chapter and verse. You looked at it carefully enough when the girls were courting.'

'The girls didn't stand to inherit,' says Jonty. 'This is more complicated.'

'Wouldn't have happened with a Yorkshire lass. Why did he break up with that Rosaline from Foxholes? He was besotted with her. All that sighing and shutting himself in his room. All those poems. What happened to her?'

Jonty looks away. 'I don't know.'

'You don't know much tonight do you, lad? What about annulment?'

'Annulment?'

'Yes,' booms the Earl. 'Annulment. Can we annul?'

156

'I - '

'Don't say you don't know, Jonty. You're a lawyer. It's a legal question. Can we annul? They can't have consummated. They're still dancing.'

'We can't annul by proxy,' says Jonty. 'And it's not just a legal issue. Catholics don't annul. Father Rogan won't stand for it.'

'Father Rogan is a blatherskite,' booms the Earl. 'All that codswallop about the north being untamed.' He suppresses a cough. 'I'll give him untamed.'

'And there's the pre-nup.'

'Pre-nup? Pre-nup! Jonty, don't tell me you…'

'Anna insisted.'

'Who exactly is Anna?'

'Anna Sampson. The American lawyer.'

'Another Yank! They're taking over,' booms the Earl. 'Again. First it was the army, now it's lawyers and priests. What in God's name is next? They'll be wanting to turn the estate into a theme park. They'll be wanting to let the public ride the bikes. They'll be persuading Mandy Howe to fill the gift shop with Hollywood coffee mugs and keyrings and window stickers. They'll be offering star-cross'd weddings and doing concession deals with the Eoferwic Arms.'

Jonty says nothing. He's thinking about warranties and indemnities and full and frank disclosure, trying to remember what amendments Anna forced him to agree to.

Beyond the window the longest day continues.

Somewhere in the Hall the cuckoo clock sounds.

'What does it say?' asks the Earl. 'This pre-nup.'

'She keeps the title,' says Jonty.

'The title.' The Earl keeps his voice neutral. '*My* title.'

'Well, technically it won't be - '

157

'Don't give me technically, Jonty. Do not give me technically. What else?'

'Other... bits and pieces.'

'What bits and pieces?'

'The bike collection.'

A strangled sound struggles in the Earl's throat.

'And the gift shop.'

The Earl's body begins to quake and his face begins to colour.

'And marketing rights for weddings and concessions.'

The Earl's fingers clench and unclench, clutching and releasing some invisible object. Quietly he says, 'Has the time come for me to instruct a new lawyer, Jonty?'

Jonty thinks quickly. He's surprised to find he's exhilarated by the danger. Like when he was on the verge of losing the All-Yorkshire Inter-Schools Junior Chess Final. He'd made his move and at the last moment, as he was about to take his finger off his queen, he'd spotted the trap. Adrenaline had shown him a way out. Now, as then, his near miss provides him with an opportunity.

'Jonty?'

'You could disinherit,' says Jonty. 'If Oliver doesn't inherit, nothing vests in her and that clause of the pre-nup is irrelevant. There'd be nothing for it to bite on.'

'Disinherit,' says the Earl. He stands, pours another brandy. He looks at Jonty's empty glass and pointedly replaces the decanter on the tray. There's a glassy rattle as he replaces the stopper. He returns to his studded leather armchair. 'Disinherit,' he says again. 'What would that mean for the estate? For the Trust?'

'That depends on the trustees,' says Jonty. His gaze drifts from the Earl to the decanter and back again. He says, 'The deed allows the trustees to distribute as they see fit.'

'Oliver is a trustee.'

'It only needs two signatures,' says Jonty. He noses his empty glass. 'Yours and mine will suffice. As settlor you can't take anything back. But you can decide where it goes. You could reverse your decision about the distaff.'

'Share it between the girls, you mean? Like King Lear?'

'Perhaps not like Lear,' says Jonty. 'That ended badly.'

'I'm surprised you know how it ended, lad. Never one for exams, were you? Only when it suited.'

'We did it for the school play, remember? In our last year at St Peter's. JHF set it on a chess board.' Jonty noses his glass again. 'I was Edmund.' He takes a non-existent swig from the empty glass and thinks of late night rehearsals with Regan and Goneril.

The Earl grunts and coughs. He says, 'All I remember is Oliver playing the damned Fool.'

25

Oliver is alone in the Scarlet Breakfast Room. Triangles of toast are going cold in the rack.

From beyond the open door comes the sound of Izzie's voice saying, 'Lady Isabel.'

Oliver looks up.

'Lady Isabel,' she says again, closer now.

She materialises in the doorway, pauses for effect and sweeps into the room. Instantly the Scarlet Breakfast Room feels more scarlet.

'Is that right?' she says. 'Or is it Viscountess Isabel?'

'The name,' says Oliver, 'is Mundayne. Lady Mundayne.'

He gazes at his new wife with a mixture of love, and pride, and relief that the waiting is over and breakfast can begin.

His recollection of how the big day ended is hazy. Queasily he remembers laughter and a bottle on its side on the table, neck pointing towards him.

He says, 'Viscountess is only for envelopes. In person it's Lady. And a Lady is never formally addressed by her forename.'

'I'll use Markham,' says Izzie. 'Lady Markham.'

'That's not how it - '

'Or is it 'The'?' asks Izzie. 'The Lady Markham. Nick will be fuming. What's this?'

'Earl Grey,' says Oliver.

'It's cold.'

'I'll ask them to make a fresh pot. I love the smell of Earl Grey in the morning. Keeps me young.'

'It smells of museums,' says Izzie. 'That stuff they use to preserve old relics.'

She yawns.

'Tea is so… British. I need coffee.' She reaches for toast, pulls a face, pours water instead. 'So. What's everyone saying?'

'About what?' asks Oliver.

'Me, of course. I got married yesterday, remember? What are they saying about me being a Lady?'

'I haven't spoken to anyone,' says Oliver. 'I thought we could enjoy - '

'I mean the media,' says Izzie. 'No-one talks to anyone any more. No-one who's anyone.'

'Oh. I see. I never look at the papers till after breakfast. It's not good for - '

'Papers!' laughs Izzie. 'Cute. I'm not talking about media, I'm talking about *media*. As in *immediate*. Where's Brooke?'

'Shall we have breakfast first?'

'I guess you're right,' sighs Izzie. 'Brooke will be on it. He'll have nudged things along. How long before we're Earl and Countess?'

161

'A good while yet, I hope.'

'How do you mean?'

'Earldom is no great shakes,' says Oliver.

'But the sooner the better, surely?'

'My father has to die first.'

'Oh,' says Izzie. 'Can't he retire or something?'

'That's not how it works.'

'Or that thing you Brits do?' says Izzie. 'Abdicate? Like what's-his-name? Mr Simpson.'

'No. That's not how it works.'

'But I am a Viscountess?'

'In a way.' Oliver takes a piece of cold toast, smears it with butter and spoons on some marmalade. 'It's a courtesy title.'

'What does that mean?'

'It means you're not actually a Lady but you can call yourself a Lady.'

'That's crazy. Why would anyone pretend to be something they're not? How do you know which Ladies are real?'

'It's not pretence,' says Oliver. 'It's entitlement.'

'Entitlement.'

'Yes. Heirs are entitled to use the highest of their fathers' other titles. Spouses likewise. It's the same for heirs of heirs, except they have an asterisk. Until the heir inherits from the incumbent, that is. Then the heir's heir can drop the asterisk. Or pass it on to the heir's heir's heir.'

'Entitlement,' Izzie says again. 'So I am a Lady?'

'No-o,' says Oliver. 'But you're entitled to call yourself one.'

'Whatever,' says Izzie, waving away the complication. 'So long as Nick has to call me Lady. So long as the paps have to call me Lady.'

162

'Does it matter?' asks Oliver. 'What's in a name? That which - '

'Everything!' says Izzie. 'Ask Brooke. It's all about the brand.'

'Oh my word! Look at that!' Oliver points to the fig tree in the courtyard outside the breakfast room window.

'What is it?'

'A nightingale. You don't see many of those this far north.'

'What was eating the Earl?' asks Izzie. 'Yesterday. The Countess was very sweet but he was being a grouse.'

'I didn't notice,' says Oliver. 'He seemed the same as usual.'

'Did you see him in church? He looked like he was having a stroke.'

'Probably peeved that you're a Catholic.'

'What does that have to do with anything?'

'Family history,' says Oliver. 'It's a long story.'

'He didn't say a word during the whole of dinner.'

'He never talks while he's eating,' says Oliver. 'It gives him wind.'

Izzie says, 'When they cleared the tables he went off with Jonty. Some sort of meeting.'

'Probably planning to cut me off,' says Oliver.

'What does that mean?'

'Disinherit me,' says Oliver. 'Us, that is.'

'But he can't do that, right?'

Oliver shrugs. 'I don't know. Who cares? The estate's a liability anyway. Not having it will save us a fortune.'

He butters another piece of toast.

'What about the title?' asks Izzie. 'Surely he can't cancel that? It must be hereditary? Like DNA?'

'I don't know,' Oliver says again. 'That would be funny, wouldn't it? If we were plain old Mr & Mrs.'

'Surely he can't do that?'

'I'll ask Jonty. He's the expert on these things.'

Izzie says, 'If it's disinheritance or divorce - '

'Don't worry,' says Oliver. 'I'm not going anywhere. I choose you every time.' He reaches across the table for Izzie's hand.

Izzie reaches for a piece of toast that she doesn't want.

A head appears round the door. 'Everything alright?'

'Could we have a pot of coffee, please,' says Oliver. 'And a fresh pot of Earl Grey.'

'Righto. The head withdraws.'

'Don't worry,' Oliver says again. 'We'll be fine. I love you.'

He gestures at the hotplates waiting on the sideboard.

'Shall we help ourselves?'

26

'Why didn't you say anything?' asks Izzie.

Jonty says nothing. He's overwhelmed by deja vu.

'Jonty?'

'I don't kn- ' He stops himself. 'There's nothing to say. This is the first chance I've had.'

'Which?' says Izzie. 'They're two completely different things.'

'The second one. It's the first chance I've had.'

'So Oliver's right?'

'To a degree.'

'What does that mean?'

'It's a legal expression.'

Izzie says, 'That doesn't answer the question.'

'That's the whole point of legal expressions,' says Jonty.

He puts his hand on Izzie's leg.

Izzie pushes it away.

Jonty says, 'It means the Earl is thinking about it.'

'But he can't do it, right?'

'I'll have to look at the Trust deed.'

'Why do you need to do that? You must know what it says by now.'

'Always go back to the document,' says Jonty. 'That's the First Law of... Law.'

'Stop avoiding the question,' demands Izzie. 'Tell me what's going on.'

Jonty sighs. 'The Earl is concerned. He summoned me to his office.'

'You already told me that.'

'He wanted to disinherit.'

'So Oliver is right. What did you say?'

'I argued against it. I did my level best to talk him out of it but I'm not a miracle-worker. It'll take time. He's like an oil tanker.'

'Is that one of your British what-do-you-call-its? Hockney rhyming slang?'

'Oil tanker? No,' says Jonty. 'It's an analogy. Getting the Earl to change course isn't easy. Not once he's got an idea in his head.'

From beyond the open door comes the sound of Oliver's voice saying, 'Jonty, can I - '

Oliver appears in the doorway. 'Oh, hello!'

Izzie smiles. 'I've been talking to Jonty about the Earl. Jonty is strategising.'

'Yes,' says Jonty. 'Strategising.'

Oliver looks at them. 'Strategising?'

Izzie says, 'It's a Californian thing.'

'Yes,' says Jonty. 'Strategising is the new negotiating. Anyway, I'm glad you're both here. I need to talk to you about the magazine. They're refusing to pay.'

'But we had a deal,' says Izzie. 'Half a million dollars.'

'Pounds,' says Jonty.

166

'Whatever.'

'What happened?' asks Oliver.

'Piracy,' says Jonty. 'One of the guests had a camera. Sold pictures to a rival magazine.'

'That's not down to us,' says Izzie.

'Who?' asks Oliver.

'*Hello!*' says Jonty.

'What?'

'It's a magazine. The one Michael Douglas and Catherine Zeta-Jones sued. Went to the Court of Appeal. Took seven years.'

'I know what *Hello!* is,' says Oliver. 'I meant which guest.'

Jonty looks away. 'We don't know. The pictures are credited to Anonymous Bosch.'

Oliver says, 'We didn't invite anyone called Anonymous Bosch.'

'I don't think it's a real name,' says Jonty. He straightens his tie. 'I think someone was trying to... er... cover his tracks.'

'Exactly,' says Izzie. 'So it's not down to us.'

Oliver says, '*His* tracks? How do you know he's a him?'

'Their tracks,' says Jonty. '*OK!* says it's a breach of contract. They say either it's an inside job or - '

'Inside job?' says Oliver. 'Why would we risk losing half a million pounds?'

'To double your money,' says Jonty.

'Are you saying *Hello!* paid double?'

'We don't know,' says Jonty, too loud and too fast. 'It's just a theory. *OK!* says either it's an inside job or security wasn't tight enough. They say that's a breach either way. They might have a point.'

'A point?' says Izzie. 'What point? Whose side are you on, Jonty?'

Jonty says, 'Yours of course, Izzie.'

She smiles. 'Good. So. What are we going to do?'

'Yes,' says Oliver. 'What's the way forward? What are the next steps? Should we sue this… Anonymous Bosch? Ridiculous name.'

'I think it's quite witty,' says Jonty. He straightens his tie again. 'Anyway,' he says, 'we'll never work out who's hiding behind the name. *Hello!* will protect its source.'

'How do you know that?'

'First Law of Journalism.'

'There must be someone we can sue.'

Jonty says, 'Well…'

'Yes?'

'If *OK!* sues us we could Part 20 *Hello!*'

'What the hummer does that mean?'

'It's a legal expression.'

27

'God I hate dawn calls.'

Oliver grunts.

'Fourth of July,' yawns Izzie. 'The day my ancestors broke free from yours.' She pushes back the sheet.

Oliver rolls away. He mumbles, 'It's too early for breaking free.'

'And it's wrap day,' says Izzie.

Oliver rolls towards her again. 'Eh?'

She says, 'Last day of filming, thank God.'

'It's not day yet. Nowhere near. Stay here.' He reaches towards her.

She moves away. 'Got to go see Flo. Got to be looking my best when I stab myself.' She levers herself out of bed and pulls on some loose clothes.

In the half-light Oliver watches her lift her elbows and gather her hair into a bunch. He says, 'When will I see you?'

'At the wrap party,' says Izzie. 'Hot dogs and fireworks.' She yawns again. 'God I need coffee.'

'Hot dogs?'

169

'For the Fourth,' says Izzie. 'It's not the Fourth without hot dogs.'

'The Earl's not going to like that. Smell of fried onions drifting all over the estate.'

'It's already agreed,' says Izzie. 'Jonty sorted it.'

She stretches and suddenly she's awake, energised and enthusiastic.

'Hot dogs, popcorn, star-spangled fireworks. Our castle is gonna be more American than the White House.'

* * *

'Thus - with a kiss - I die.'

Silence.

'Bellissimo,' whispers Sal. 'Bellissimo. Cut.'

'Cut!' calls the 1st AD.

Immediately the set swarms with crew. Props are re-set, lights are adjusted, mics are checked, faces are powdered.

Filming has been going on for hours. Oliver, though, has just arrived. He's still adjusting to the sepulchral dimness of the wine cellar after the summer sunshine outside. He's bewildered. He's witnessed this ritual before but here, below ground, there's something other-worldly about it. The vaulted ceilings cast unexpected shadows. The stone curves cause strange echoes. The angled lights deepen the darkness beyond. There's an intensity to the crew's work. Elves or goblins forging gold from base metal. Everyone talking in undertones. Figures detaching themselves from the darkness, fulfilling their purpose and dissolving back into the gloom. Izzie, at the heart of it, is lost in the melee.

170

At some secret signal the set clears and the scene begins again.

'A grave?' says Romeo. 'Oh no. A lantern. For here lies Juliet, and her beauty makes this vault a feasting presence full of light.'

Oliver gazes at Izzie on Sal's monitor. A single bar of light cuts across her face. The feasting presence full of light is in Romeo's mind. Oliver feels the weight of Orvane pressing down on the cool, dim vault; the pillars and buttresses pressing back.

'Oh my love, my wife!' continues Romeo. Nick looks directly into the camera; directly into Oliver's eyes as Oliver watches the monitor. 'Death, that hath sucked the honey of thy breath - ' Nick moves to Izzie's side, puts his hand tenderly to her face ' - hath no power yet upon thy beauty.' He bends and gently kisses Juliet's cheek.

Oliver is lost somewhere between Orvane and Verona.

'I will stay with thee, and never from this palace of dim night depart again.'

Somewhere between artifice in a wine cellar and limbo in the Capulet vault.

'Here will I set up my everlasting rest, and shake the yoke of the inauspicious stars from - '

A phone pings.

Heads turn.

Jonty is standing directly behind Oliver.

'Shit.'

'You!' yells Sal.

'Sorry,' says Jonty. He's standing in an acoustic sweet spot so the ping and the Shit and the Sorry all echo disproportionately while Sal's yell loses all force. Jonty

171

holds up his phone. 'Usually there's no signal down here. It's Holderness Hot Dogs. They want to know where - '

Sal raises his hand. 'Silence! Craig?'

'Still rolling.'

Sal motions Nick to continue.

' - shake the yokc of the inauspicious stars from this world-wearied flesh,' continues Nick. 'Eyes, look your last. Arms, take your last embrace. Lips, seal with a righteous kiss a dateless bargain to engrossing death.'

He kisses Izzie's lifeless lips.

Jonty stifles a cough.

Oliver watches Nick extract a flask from the inside pocket of his jacket.

He hears Romeo's line about a pilot running a ship onto the rocks.

He thinks, Sail with me over these spirited waves.

He watches Nick drink from the flask.

'Thus – with a kiss – I die.'

Romeo dies.

28

Sal begins. He says, 'When, in the course of human events.'

An inebriated roar goes up. A mix of patriotic cheers and cynical jeers.

The words make Sal feel presidential. A Commander-in-Chief. His chest swells. His jaw sets. His shoulders broaden.

He looks around himself - at his cast and crew assembled before him, at the Grand Ballroom to his right and the West Terrace to his left, at the church tower beyond the Terrace and the trees, at himself at the nexus of it all - and he thinks, I was right. Orvane was the making of this movie. Orvane and Spurn. Faded grandeur and magnificent desolation. David would have settled for the back lot. David would have settled for CGI. But I am not David. I persevered and I was right. Orvane - veni, vidi, video. And now, arrivederci.

Sal thinks, David would like to be the one standing here, on this podium, about to give this speech.

But David is elsewhere.

Only I am here.

Sal thinks, How would I film the speech I'm about to give?

Or, rather, the speech I've just begun. My combined Independence/Wrap Day speech.

He imagines a crane shot beginning in the glazed dome of the double height ballroom, sweeping down, skirting the crystal chandelier, skimming the heads of the crowd, lifting again and pulling back to emphasise the isolation of the director, the leader, alone and heroic on the makeshift podium that straddles the threshold of the French windows between ballroom and terrace.

Between.

Always between.

The figure at the lectern is spotlit, surveying his domain and his personnel. On one side of the podium the noisy, crowded ballroom, skilfully lit to give the impression of myriad candles softly flickering; on the other, the terrace, peopled with smokers and hot dog wagons and popcorn stands, flaming torches supplementing the dying glow of the mid-summer sun.

And at the interface, Masuccio Salernitano.

Sal thinks, David would pace back and forth. I will be still.

He taps the twin microphones and repeats his opening line. 'When, in the course of human events.'

The evening sighs - a subtle exchange of air between inside and out, bringing the ballroom scent of perspiration and perfume and floor polish onto the terrace and introducing the terrace scent of popcorn and fried onions and cigarette smoke to the ballroom.

Jonty says, 'Smells like Hull Fair.'

174

Not enough diesel and steam for Hull Fair, thinks Oliver. He says, 'Craven Park, more like.'

He and Jonty are standing with Izzie and Flo. The four of them have been pushed by the crowd into a tight group between the makeshift bar and the inglenook fireplace.

The Earl and Countess look down on them from the Mundayne family portrait above the mantel.

'Craven Park?' says Jonty. 'Haven't been for years.'

Izzie asks, 'What's that? Baseball?'

Jonty laughs. He winks at Flo, twists and leans, right knee raised, left arm low, elbow out. His pitching arm connects with someone at the bar behind him, spilling punch. A pink stain spreads steadily over the linen. 'Sorry, sorry,' says Jonty. He holds up both hands. 'Sorry. Strike One!'

Oliver says, 'Rugby league, actually. Hull KR. The Earl was club chairman, years ago. Resigned because he couldn't stand the smell of onions.'

Someone shushes them.

They turn dutifully towards Sal, on the podium.

The room is filled with half-familiar faces. Faces Oliver recognises but knows nothing about. Faces he's seen milling about the tail-gates of trucks, stepping in and out of Winnebagos, drinking coffee from styrofoam cups, marshalling equipment, performing, pointing, building monuments, jotting down notes. Without their clipboards and tool belts and costumes and make up their familiarity is alien to him. Am I alien to them? he thinks. He feels alien to himself. He looks into his own eyes in the oil painting above the fireplace, standing awkwardly with the Earl and Countess and his elder sisters. He imagines his younger self looking out of the painting, into the eyes of his current self, and thinks, Have I always been outside myself, looking in?

Sal is talking about pulling together, shared goals, journey's end. 'It's a wrap!' he says.

Cheers from those standing closest to him; the inner circle.

'It's in the can!'

Appreciative nods from the outer circle.

'But,' says Sal, 'no journey ends at its destination.'

Agreement in the inner circle, confusion in the outer circle, indifference on the periphery.

'And,' he says, 'no journey begins with its first step.'

More agreement, more confusion, more indifference.

'Arrival and departure,' says Sal. 'Departure and arrival. The beginning and the end, the end and the beginning. Alpha and omega. What are they, these things? They are just words. They are mere concepts. They are illusions. Illusions! Every journey starts before it begins and every journey continues after its end. Every journey is a continuum. We have completed our journey but we are still travelling. We are in transition. We are... between. In an intermediate zone. On a journey between journeys.'

Flo says, 'You ok?'

'Just thinking,' says Oliver.

They watch Simone make her way towards them through the crowd, with Julian and Abram in tow.

'Evening all!' says Simone, raising both hands in greeting. 'Oops.' She brushes at the champagne she's spilt on her dress.

Someone shushes her.

'How's life over here in the intermediate zone?' says Simone, a semitone lower but no quieter. 'How were your journeys between journeys?'

176

'Too fast,' says Flo.

'Too slow,' says Izzie.

Simone says, 'In many ways a journey is as fast or as slow as you make it.'

'It's been a blast,' says Julian to Oliver. 'An absolute blast. Abram has been a star.' He puts a hand on Abram's shoulder. 'We'd have been lost without him.'

'Evening, Abram,' says Oliver. He hesitates, then raises his glass to Abram.

Abram nods acknowledgement. 'How do.'

Julian asks Oliver, 'Are you interested in future projects? Here, that is. Orvane.'

He makes an expansive gesture that takes in the ballroom and the hall and the estate.

He says, 'Simone's model was a work of art. Seems a shame not to use it again.'

Oliver says, 'The Earl might not - '

'We certainly are,' interrupts Jonty. 'Text me.' He mimes texting. 'My phone is always on.'

'So we noticed,' says Julian.

On the podium Sal is meandering towards a conclusion. Inner circle aside, the room is treating his speech as background noise; as if, Sal thinks, he were POTUS addressing the nation from a television mounted on the wall in the corner of a bar in Hicksville. Off set, no one is obliged to listen to him. It's not as easy as he'd hoped, combining a Fourth of July oration with a wrap-party speech. There are differing requirements. He reverts to the Declaration of Independence. 'We hold these truths to be self-evident,' he says. 'That all men are created equal; - '

(someone shouts, 'What about women?')

177

' - all *people* are created equal,' he says, 'that they are endowed by their Creator with certain inalienable rights; that among these are life, liberty and the pursuit of happiness - '

A huge cheer erupts. Glasses are raised.

Sal decides to cut his losses. That's as good a place as any to leave it. The pursuit of happiness.

He steps down from the podium and accepts a drink from the 1st AD.

Someone bumps Oliver's shoulder. Instinctively he thrusts his glass forward and bends at the waist, successfully redirecting the spillage from his dinner jacket to his shoes.

'Oops. Sorry, Romeo.'

'Nick,' says Izzie.

'Dizzie,' says Nick. He sniffs.

'That's Lady Markham to you.'

'You sure about that?' says Nick.

'Totally sure,' says Izzie. 'Two hundred per cent. *My* Earl is a proper earl.'

'Not yet.'

'He will be.' She puts her arm round Oliver, leans into him. 'It's in the blood, Nick. You can't just fake it with a surname.'

Nick looks at them, drains his champagne, takes another from a passing tray. He says, 'Weren't you listening to Sal? All people are created equal.'

'Some of us are more equal than others, Nick.'

'Says who?'

Oliver says, 'I think it was - '

'Henry Ford,' says Izzie.

Nick sniffs. 'Henry Ford said that?'

'Check the *Hollywood Reporter*,' says Izzie. 'It's Lady Markham.'

Nick extracts his phone from his pocket. He smiles. 'We'll see.'

'There's only one fake aristocrat round here,' says Izzie, 'and that's you.'

'Obviously the *Reporter* hasn't heard the news,' says Nick. He looks pointedly at his screen.

'What news?' asks Izzie.

Nick says, 'Must be the time difference.'

'What news, Nick?'

'Chichi Boo has been talking to the Earl,' says Nick. 'The actual Earl. She knows where it's at. She's got her finger on the pulse. The inside track. Check out the *Yorkshire Post*.'

He holds up his phone.

Izzie leans in.

Nick turns the phone away.

He says, 'There are pictures.'

He makes a show of scrolling down.

Izzie leans in again.

Again Nick turns the phone away from her.

'I know they're here someplace. Ah, here we are.'

He holds up a grainy snatch shot of Oliver and Izzie on the terrace earlier in the evening.

Oliver says, 'Who let - '

'Shall I read you the caption?' says Nick. 'Hold on.'

He lifts the phone to eye level, rotates it, enlarges the image.

He makes a show of squinting and peering closely at the screen before reading:

Disinherited: Mr and Mrs Mundayne.

29

'I'll have his head on a plate.'

'Whose head?'

'Oliver's, of course' says Izzie. 'With puttanesca sauce.'

'Steady on,' says Jonty. His voice is muffled. 'Puttanesca sauce? That's my best friend you're talking about.'

'Some friend,' says Izzie.

'It's not Ol's fault.'

'I meant you,' says Izzie. 'In bed with his wi - i - ife.'

'Bed is different,' says Jonty, emerging, sweating, from under the sheet. 'All's fair in love and law.'

'Is that what this is?' says Izzie. 'Love?'

'It's a phrase,' says Jonty. 'Something I learned in... never mind.'

The window is open. The breeze brings the summer afternoon into the room. Jonty arranges the pillow against the headboard, sits up, lights a cigarette. He takes a drag and passes it to Izzie.

'Thanks,' says Izzie. 'So. What do we do?'

'About us?'

'Us? No. About my title of course.'

'Oh.'

'We need a plan, Jonty.'

'We?'

'Yes, we. Us. You're my lawyer, aren't you? You know about these things. Or have you suddenly spotted a conflict of interest? Do I need to call Anna?'

'There's no need to call Anna.'

'Good,' says Izzie.

'I can handle this,' says Jonty. 'It's what I trained for.'

'Good,' says Izzie again. 'As long as you know where your loyalties lie.'

'What do you want?' asks Jonty. He thinks, What do I want?

'What do you mean?'

'What do you want to achieve? What's your goal?'

'I want my title back. I won't have Nick Earl getting the better of me. You saw the way he and Ellen were strutting round that ballroom. Like peacocks. He was loving it.'

'So which is it?' asks Jonty. 'The title or revenge?'

'They go hand in hand, Jonty. Surely you can see that? Hand in hand.'

'What about Oliver?'

Izzie says, 'What about him?'

'Do you want to keep him, too?'

'This isn't about Oliver. It's about my title. My entitlement.'

'OK,' says Jonty. 'Right.'

Izzie passes back the cigarette.

Jonty accepts it, makes to take a drag, changes his mind. He stubs it out in a saucer on the bedside cabinet. He says, 'Has Oliver said anything about it?'

'About what?'

'Being disinherited.'

'He said the estate is a liability,' says Izzie. 'Said it would save us a fortune not having it.'

'And what did he say about the title?'

'He said he doesn't care about the title. He said he never has. He started quoting my own lines at me.'

'Lines?'

'Sal's screenplay,' says Izzie. 'What's in a name? and all that.'

'A rose by any other name would still be a rose?'

'Would smell as sweet,' corrects Izzie. 'So Romeo would, were he not Romeo called, retain that dear perfection which he owes without that title.'

'Wise words,' says Jonty.

'Wise words my ass. It's all about the brand. Retain perfection without that title? How would that work? Nobody who's anybody is anything without their brand. Whose side are you on?'

'Yours, Izzie, yours.' He rolls towards her, nestles into the pillows, puts his hand on her belly.

'Oliver said he loves me whether I'm Izzie or Isabel or Lady or Mrs.' She moves Jonty's hand lower. 'He said he doesn't care about any of that so long as he's with me.' She sighs, 'Yes, there. Right there. He said he couldn't live without me.'

Jonty stills his hand. 'He said what?'

'He said he couldn't live without me.' She nudges herself against Jonty's touch.

Jonty retrieves his hand, sits upright. He says, 'That's it.'

'That's it?'

'The answer,' says Jonty. 'You just have to die.'

'A title is no use if I'm dead.'

'Not for real,' says Jonty. 'Like Juliet.'

'I'm done with Juliet.'

'But that's the solution,' says Jonty. 'Think about it. What is it you say to Tom Waits when you think you've lost Romeo.'

'I tell him I'll stab myself in the heart if he doesn't help me. Or leap from the battlements.'

'I've had clients like that.'

'Really?'

'Well, not personally,' says Jonty. 'But I've read about them on clientsfromhell.com. Anyway, Tom Waits says don't kill yourself, just fake it.'

'And?' says Izzie. 'How does that help?'

'It's Sunday,' says Jonty.

'Stop talking in riddles.'

'You're not disinherited yet,' says Jonty. 'The Earl hasn't formalised it. He's announced it but he hasn't - ' Jonty mimes signing ' - signed on the dotted line.'

Jonty is pleased with himself. He smiles at the ceiling again.

'And...?'

'And he won't,' says Jonty. 'Not till tomorrow at the earliest. Probably Tuesday. And he might be dead by then. He doesn't like doing paperwork on a Monday. He likes to ease into the week. He needs me, and he needs an independent witness, and he needs a pen. This is Eoferwic How. He can't get those things on a Sunday.'

'And...?'

'So that gives us a couple of days to set something up. If he dies, no problem. And if he doesn't, you do. Then he'll have no reason to sign. No reason to disinherit.'

'He'll have even more reason when I come back to life.'

'Not if he's dead,' says Jonty. 'He hasn't got long left. A matter of days. Weeks, maybe. All you have to do is die and then lie low for a couple of weeks. We could go away. I know a nice little place in the Dales. Near Masham. We could visit the Black Sheep brewery. We could go to the Cheese Experience at Hawes and watch them make Wensleydale.' He mimes eating cheese.

'A couple of weeks!' says Izzie. 'Can't we just bump him off?'

'No,' says Jonty. 'Absolutely not. We can't go round bumping people off. That would be... wrong. It's probably a breach of the Solicitors' Code of Conduct. I could be struck off.'

'But I can't disappear for weeks on end,' says Izzie. 'I've got a movie to promote.'

'Bit early for that isn't it? You've only just finished filming. Half the crew are still sleeping it off in the Eoferwic Arms. Most of the trucks are still parked in the Old Orchard.'

'Not this movie,' says Izzie. 'The last one. Jane Eyre. Show business is a treadmill. I can't promote a movie if I'm dead.'

'Death is perfect publicity,' says Jonty. 'They'll come flocking. Look. Do you want to be a Lady or not?'

Izzie says, 'I want to be a Lady.'

'Well then.'

'So what's it to be?' asks Izzie. 'I can't exactly leap from the battlements.'

184

'No,' says Jonty. 'No leaping or stabbing. What about a sleeping potion?'

'No one's going to believe that,' says Izzie. 'No one.'

'It worked for Shakespeare.'

'This isn't Shakespeare.'

Jonty says, 'We could leave a pile of clothes at Spurn Head.'

'We already did that, remember? It was hellish cold.'

'Hell is supposed to be hot,' says Jonty. 'Anyway, I didn't notice the cold.'

'Says the man who kept his socks on.'

'I mean, stage a drowning,' says Jonty. 'Like Lord Lucan.'

'Lord who?'

'The 7th Earl of Lucan. He disappeared near a beach. They found his car. It's the aristocratic thing to do.'

30

'Take thou this vial and this distilléd liquor drink thou off.'

Friar Lawrence's line hangs in the half dark, a guttural growl in the gloom.

The edit suite is thirty-three floors up, but the unchanging twenty-four hour chill of the windowless air-conditioned room gives it an underground feel. Furtive, technological: a surveillance bunker. The air is tainted with the electronic tinge of hot plastic and ozone. In eternal twilight, in high-backed leather chairs, sit Sal and the editor, Sven 'Mack' Myra.

From the bank of monitors more words emerge:

' - through all thy veins shall run a cold and drowsy humour - '

(Tom Waits's shamanic eyes narrow and glisten)

' - no pulse shall keep his native progress, no warmth, no breath shall testify thou livest - '

(Sal signals Mack to call up an even tighter shot - Izzie's double reflection in Waits's rheumy eyes)

' - and in this borrowed likeness of shrunk death thou shalt continue two and forty hours.'

There's a double knock.

Light floods the room.

Sal says, 'What the - ' He keeps his eyes on the monitor.

Anna enters. Campanile follows. Twilight reasserts itself.

'We're working here,' says Sal.

Mack hits pause.

Sal turns. 'I will not have my movie ruined by interruptions. I will not - ' He sees Campanile's face. 'David. What is it?'

Campanile says, 'Mack. A moment, please.'

Mack exits.

'We've been trying to get hold of you,' says Campanile.

'The edit is a phone-free zone, David. You know that. There's a sign on the door.'

'What are you doing in the edit?' says Campanile.

'Editing?'

'You've only been back five minutes.'

'Less than that,' says Sal. 'I'm still at LAX. I'm still catching up with myself. Only part of me is here.' (Campanile notices Sal is barefoot, flexing his toes.) 'I'm in transition, David. Between zones. But I had to review Tom's scenes. I had no choice. His agent has been on my back. As soon as we touched down, messages. My inbox. Full of messages. People think it's easy, being a director. They think it's all red carpets and tuxedos. But it's not, David. It's not. Let me tell you. It's redeyes and text messages. Tom is a genius. A genius! But his agent, David. His agent is - '

'Doing his job,' says Anna.

Campanile says, 'Sal. We've been trying to get hold of you for a reason.'

'But Tom's agent - '

'It's important,' says Campanile. He looks at Anna.

Anna says, 'Izzie is missing.'

The whirr of the air conditioning.

'Missing,' echoes Sal.

'Missing,' repeats Anna.

'Missing how?' asks Sal.

'Missing as in, Presumed Dead,' says Anna. 'There are helicopters. Search and rescue.'

'Presumed alive, then?' says Sal.

Campanile says, 'There were clothes on the beach.'

'What beach?'

'Spurn Head,' says Campanile. 'Your beach, Sal. Mantua. Unfenced existence, you called it.'

'Don't blame me for this, David. Philip Larkin called it that, not me. This is not my fault. Izzie's clothes are not my responsibility.'

'I don't care about Philip Larkin,' says Campanile. 'I don't care about British painters, period. If you hadn't insisted on Spurn Head - '

'Children, please,' says Anna.

'How long?' asks Sal.

Anna says, 'Forty-two hours.'

'Forty-two hours! And they've only just told us?'

'The Mundaynes tried to keep it quiet,' says Anna. 'But that columnist got wind of it. Hazel Byrne.'

Sal says, 'Hazel Byrne is not the columnist. The columnist had a porn star name.'

'Her real name is Hazel Byrne,' says Anna. 'She had pictures of the clothes on the beach. Neatly folded. There

188

was a hire car in the parking lot. She had pictures of that, too.'

'What are the chances?' asks Sal. 'After forty-two hours?'

'Slim,' says Anna. 'It's the North Sea. There are currents.' She sits heavily in Mack's chair.

Sal crosses himself. 'O lamentable day! O heavy day. Alack the day! Like an untimely frost upon the sweetest flower of all the field. She's - I can't speak.' He continues to speak. 'Accurséd, unhappy, wretched, hateful day! Most miserable hour that e'er time saw. O woe! O woeful, woeful, woeful day! O hateful day! Never was seen so black a day as this.' He stops.

The whirr of the air conditioning fills the silence.

Anna says, 'David?'

Campanile has wandered into the no man's land between the control console and the bank of monitors. His fingers are pressed against the glass of the key monitor; pressed against Izzie's face, freeze-framed in another time and place. With his back to Anna and Sal he says, 'Is this down to me?'

Anna says, 'For God's sake, David! Get a grip. Not everything is about you.'

'Like an untimely frost,' says Campanile.

He turns and his suit turns with him.

He's silhouetted against the glow of Izzie's image on the monitor.

'I should never have agreed to a tragedy. Anna, why did you let me agree to a tragedy? You should have advised against a tragedy. A tragedy was always going to end in tears. I don't want tears. Belltower is not about tears. I want happiness. We should have done something less... tragic. We should have done something more gentle. Something frivolous.'

Part of his mind starts to consider the connotations of the word frivolous but it doesn't seem important.

He says, 'We should have done The Winter's Tale. Sal, why Romco & Juliet? Why not The Winter's Tale?'

Part Three

31

'What's this?'

'A contract.'

'I can see it's a contract, Izzie. It says "Contract" at the top.'

'Well then.' Izzie sits.

'What are you showing it to me for?'

'Because you're involved, Jonty.'

'I am not "involved".' Jonty draws the inverted commas in the air. 'Film deals are Brooke's domain.'

'Movie deals,' says Izzie.

Jonty says, 'Whatever.' He slurps from an oversized mug of tea. 'Brooke won't stand for me treading on his toes.'

'You're not treading on his toes.' Izzie slides the contract across the kitchen table towards Jonty. 'He's on the other side of the ocean.'

'Not his literal toes.' Jonty slides the contract back. 'If I start stepping into his shoes he's not going to stand for it. He doesn't strike me as the type who'll take that sort of thing lying down.'

'He thinks I'm dead, remember?' Izzie slides the contract half way across the table. 'Anyway, I pay for his shoes.'

'So let him deal with your contract wrangles.' Jonty slides the contract part way back. 'In due course, that is. When the time comes. After you come back to life. We can't do anything til then.'

'Exactly,' says Izzie. 'That's why I need you to look at this.'

'It's not my domain.'

'It's not a movie contract. It's unusual.'

Beyond the kitchen window summer continues.

Jonty sighs. 'What's unusual about it?'

'It's an assassination contract,' says Izzie. 'For a hit.'

'Of course!' says Jonty. 'A hit. Silly me. Who's the target? The prime minister? That president of yours?'

Izzie says, 'The name isn't filled in yet. There's a box. You write the name in the box. Or names. They've got a deal on - buy one get one free.'

'Filled in?' says Jonty. 'Is that another joke?'

'It's not a joke, Jonty. I've been dead long enough. A matter of days, you said - a couple of weeks. It's been nearly a month.'

'That is a matter of days,' says Jonty. 'Twenty-four, to be precise. We've been enjoying ourselves haven't we? Having fun?'

He reaches across the table for Izzie's hand but she keeps it in her lap.

He says, 'The Cheese Experience was a revelation. Those plastic hats.'

'Dying was easy,' says Izzie. 'I'm very good at dying. Lucy died, Kathy died, Juliet died. I've had a lot of practice.'

196

'Well then,' says Jonty.

'Being dead is different. It's killing me.'

'Do you want a cup of tea?' He holds up his mug.

'Disguising myself every time I go outside. Being someone else all the time.'

'Isn't that what you do? Hollywood stars?'

'I can't do anything while I'm dead, Jonty. It has to stop. What's the plan?'

Jonty says, 'The plan.'

'Yes, the plan. You got me into this. How do I get out? How do I resurrect myself?'

'Ah,' says Jonty. 'The exit strategy. Yes. I don't know. You were caught in a rip tide, so…' He tails off.

'You're supposed to have a plan, Jonty. Isn't that what you do? Attorneys?'

'Lawyers,' says Jonty.

'Isn't that what you're supposed to do? Think ahead? All that chess.'

'Sometimes one has to improvise,' says Jonty. 'Play it by ear. Go with the flow.'

'How did Lucas do it?'

'Who?'

'Lord Lucas. How did he come back to life?'

'Lucan,' says Jonty. 'He didn't. He's still dead. Or not. He's been sighted more times than Elvis. So. Rip tide. You cling to your body board. You're washed ashore at Withernsea - '

'I don't have a body board.'

'Nobody needs to know that.'

'I've never been body boarding.'

'No wonder you got into trouble then,' says Jonty. 'So. You're washed ashore at Withernsea. You can't remember anything. Total blank. Someone takes you in. One day

197

you visit the Lighthouse Museum and when you see the Kay Kendall exhibition you remember you're a film star.'

'Who?'

'Kay Kendall. She was a 50s film star. She was born in Withernsea and there are exhibits in the Lighthouse Museum. Film stills, posters, memorabilia. Her fans come flocking.'

'I mean who took me in?' says Izzie.

'Let's not worry about the details. Everyone will be so pleased to have you back no one will bother about the details.'

'They'll be all over the details,' says Izzie. 'They'll want to make a movie out of the details. They'll want me to play myself. Imagine it, Jonty. Lady Isabel Markham as Lady Isabel Markham. Lady Isabel Markham *is* Lady Isabel Markham.'

'All over the details,' says Jonty. 'Right. Well. Let's be honest, then.'

'Honest?'

'-ish,' says Jonty. 'Honest-ish. We'll blame the press. We'll say you needed a break from all the attention. This was the only way to avoid the intrusion. We'll leave out the bit about the Earl.'

'OK,' says Izzie. 'Honest-ish it is. But first we need to move things on.'

'Move things on?'

'Yes. I can't come back to life till the Earl... moves on.'

Jonty says, 'We - you - have to be patient. He hasn't got long.'

'That's what you said a month ago.'

'Twenty-four days.'

'Whatever. He's still here. He needs a nudge.'

198

'What do you mean by "nudge"?' Jonty starts to raise his hands to draw the inverted commas but changes his mind.

Izzie nods again at the contract.

'You're not serious?' Jonty glances at the cover sheet.

Izzie extends her right hand, places the tips of three fingers against the bottom edge of the contract and slides it to Jonty's side of the table. Her little finger and thumb remain aloof.

'Oh my God,' says Jonty. 'You really mean it.' He reads the contract, sits back, looks at Izzie. 'Where did you get this?'

'It doesn't matter,' says Izzie.

'It does matter.'

She says, 'Someone I know in LA. Someone who owes me a favour.'

'So someone knows you're alive?'

'He doesn't care if I'm alive or dead,' says Izzie. 'He never did.'

'Some friend.'

'I didn't say he's a friend,' says Izzie. 'I said he's someone I know. Anyway, he doesn't know I'm me. I used a synonym.'

'Pseudonym.'

'Whatever.'

'If he doesn't know you're you,' says Jonty, 'how does he know he's returning a favour?'

Izzie says, 'He doesn't. Yet.'

'The Earl's not going to like it. A hitman trampling all over the estate.'

'The Earl won't know,' says Izzie. 'Hitmen don't announce themselves.'

'Still,' says Jonty.

199

'Think about it. All that coughing.'

Jonty coughs. 'What does coughing have to do with murder?'

'I wouldn't call it murder,' says Izzie. 'He's suffering. Anyone can see that. I thought he was having a stroke at the wedding. It can't be nice. You said yourself he's not got long left. We'd be doing him a favour.'

'We?'

'We're in this together, Jonty. You're involved.'

'I'm not "involved".' This time Jonty raises both palms and leans back in his chair. 'It's your title. I'm just your legal advisor.'

'I see,' says Izzie. 'Just my legal advisor. You attorneys are all the same - '

Lawyers,' says Jonty.

'Whatever. You're all the same. Happy to dole out advice - if the price is right - but you never put it into action. You never take responsibility for it.'

'That's what advice is,' says Jonty. 'And my advice is to do nothing. I'm happy to put that into action.'

'And watch him suffer?' says Izzie. 'We'd be doing him a favour.'

'It's only a favour if it's what he wants. If it's his choice. Even then it's illegal.'

Izzie says, 'What about Oliver, then?'

'What about Oliver?'

'He's unhappy.'

'He's grieving,' says Jonty. 'For you. He'll be fine when you come back to life. What are you suggesting?'

Izzie says, 'We're still married aren't we? Me and him?'

'Yes,' says Jonty. 'You're missing, not dead. Officially speaking.'

'And he's still the heir?'

'Yes,' says Jonty. 'I was right - when you disappeared the Earl decided he didn't need to sign.'

'So if Oliver does a Romeo the title's mine,' says Izzie. 'Which means if you play your cards right you could be Earl.'

'What are you saying?'

'I'm saying, if you object to helping the Earl along, what about helping Oliver along?'

'You mean...? No,' says Jonty. 'No. No, no no. I can't do that. There's history. They've been good to me. They treat me like family. An insider.'

'You're telling me you've never thought about being Earl?' says Izzie. 'All those years. You've never wondered what it would be like? You've never imagined a plaster cast of you in that church with all the others? You've never thought about being someone who's someone?'

'Of course not,' says Jonty. He straightens his tie. 'Of course... not. Those effigies are alabaster, by the way.'

'Whatever.'

'Anyway,' says Jonty, 'helping a terminally ill person is one thing. What you've just suggested would be a step too far.'

'So you agree?' says Izzie. 'We can help the Earl?'

'That's not what I said.'

'I've already paid the deposit,' says Izzie. 'Half up front just to see the contract. So a name has to go in that box.'

32

'D~ram?'

'Of poison?'

'Restorative,' says Jonty. 'There's a reason they call it water of life. *Uisge be'atha*. It's Latin for - '

'It's Gaelic,' says Oliver. His voice is flat. 'And whisky just means water. It's the other bit that means "of life".'

'Whatever,' says Jonty.

'You sound like Izzie.'

Jonty says, 'Do you want a dram or not?'

Oliver sighs. 'Alright. Corryvreckan.'

Jonty nods. He levers himself out of his chair and crosses to the drinks cabinet.

'Romeo pays forty ducats for his,' says Oliver.

'Forty pieces of silver?'

'If you're referring to Judas, that was thirty.'

'Forty's a bit steep, then.' Jonty pours two generous drams. 'Romeo should have haggled. Or got me to haggle for him.'

'Romeo's wasn't blood money. Not like Judas. Romeo's was an inducement. To encourage the apothecary to do him a favour.'

'That's illegal,' says Jonty. 'Bribery Act 2010.' There's a glassy rattle as he puts the stopper back in the decanter.

Oliver says, 'Let me have a dram of poison, such soon-speeding gear as will disperse itself through all the veins.'

'Here', says Jonty. 'Disperse this through your veins. It'll make you feel better.'

'I don't want to feel better,' says Oliver. 'Better would be a betrayal.'

'Of what?' Jonty sinks back into the studded leather armchair opposite Oliver.

'Of whom,' says Oliver. 'Izzie. Who else? Romeo didn't drink to feel better. He drank to join Juliet.'

Jonty says, 'Soon-speeding gear sounds pretty life-affirming to me.' He noses, sips, holds his glass up to the light. 'God, that's good.'

Oliver stares out of the window. He completes the quote. 'Disperse itself through all the veins that the weary life-taker may fall dead.'

'Oh,' says Jonty. 'You're not thinking of...?'

'I don't know,' says Oliver. 'I don't know.'

'She's missing,' says Jonty. 'Not…'

The clock ticks.

'Dead?' says Oliver. He sips his dram. 'Four weeks? In the North Sea?'

'Twenty-four days,' says Jonty.

Oliver looks at the clock. 'If you want to be pedantic it's three weeks, three days, three hours and thirty-three minutes, give or take a few seconds.'

'From when?'

'From the time she Paid and Displayed. It's on the parking ticket.'

Jonty says, 'Things are not always what they seem.'

'What's that supposed to mean?'

'She might turn up,' says Jonty. 'Elsewhere. She might have been carried somewhere. By the tide.'

Oliver snorts. 'So long as it's this side of the Humber. Can't have her turning up in Lincolnshire.'

'I'm serious,' says Jonty. 'She might have been washed up. Not remember who she is.'

'Don't be ridiculous.'

'Who knows?' says Jonty. 'Stranger things have happened.'

'Like what?'

'That American reporter,' says Jonty. 'They found her in Alaska the year we left St Peter's, remember? Twelve years after she disappeared. She couldn't remember who she was. Fugue state, they called it.'

'Twelve years!' says Oliver. 'I can't live twelve years without her, Jonty. Not being with her is like banishment. Exile. And exile from Izzie is more terrifying than death.'

'Stop saying the D-word.'

'Alright,' says Oliver, 'nothingness. Nothingness would be easier. It would be peaceful. Calm. Abram said something to me the other day.'

Jonty says, 'He speaks?'

'Yes,' says Oliver. 'Wise words, actually.'

'Thus spake Singleton?'

'It's easy to mock,' says Oliver. 'He was trying to help. It was an odd phrase he used. The right to remain unconceived.'

'The what?'

'He said conception is where the trouble begins.'

204

Jonty noses his Corryvreckan, takes another sip. 'What, the alignment of the stars when the cells start dividing? Everything mapped out?'

'No,' says Oliver. 'The principle. No one asks if we want to be born. We're not consulted.'

Jonty laughs. 'That would be some consultation. Imagine the attendance note!'

'Lawyers,' says Oliver. 'You're so literal. We're conceived whether we like it or not, Jonty. And we're born helpless. We rely on an omnipotent other. That conditions us for life. We learn to accept what we're dealt. We believe there's a Dealer.'

'Some accept,' says Jonty. 'Some act.'

'What do you mean by that?'

'Some let things happen, others make things happen.'

'This is because of the title,' says Oliver. 'It's because of what I am. What is it Romeo says? As if that name did murder her.'

'Stop quoting that bloody play,' says Jonty. 'It's not helping. Anyway, Izzie is not dead.'

Shit.

Jonty feels Oliver's eyes on him.

He says, 'What I mean is - '

'You don't know that, Jonty. Nobody knows that. If she's not dead, where is she? The title is a curse. It's because of the title.'

'It's because of the tide,' says Jonty. 'It's not your fault. It's chance, not destiny.'

'Same thing,' says Oliver. 'Anyway, that's easy for you to say. You're not caught up in it. You're not... involved.'

'I'm here, aren't I?'

'But you're not me, Jonty. You're not destined to be Earl. You're an outsider. That title has been hanging over me my whole life. That... label. Boxing me in, defining me - or defining what I will be, one day. I can't be what I am because of what I will be. You don't know what it's like, Jonty. Not knowing who you are. Or knowing who you are but having to be someone else. And then Izzie. She was the only one who saw me for who I am.'

'An outsider?' says Jonty.

'What?'

'You said I'm an outsider.'

'You know what I mean.'

'Yes,' says Jonty, 'I think I do.'

Beyond the window night falls.

'Do you really think it's because of the tide?' says Oliver. 'Pure chance?'

Jonty says nothing.

'If it's not my fault why do I feel guilt? I should follow her. Like Romeo follows Juliet.'

'For God's sake!' says Jonty. 'Snap out of it. You're not Romeo and she's not Juliet.'

He stands, takes Oliver's glass, returns to the drinks cabinet.

Quietly, with his back to Oliver, he says, 'Sorry.'

Oliver says to Jonty's back, 'I can't do it myself, Jonty. Follow her. I need your help.'

Jonty pours two more drams, hands Oliver his glass returns to his chair. He says, 'Following her is illegal. Helping is illegal.'

Oliver says, 'I'm not asking for legal advice. We're conceived without consent. We're born without consent. So we have the right to redress. Nothingness regained.'

'Abram Singleton's words?'

206

'My conclusion,' says Oliver. 'It makes it bearable. Knowing there's a way out.'

'Knowing there's an emergency exit is one thing,' says Jonty. 'Using it is another. Wait. See how things pan out. That's my advice.'

'As a lawyer or a friend?'

'Both,' says Jonty.

'But she's gone, Jonty. She's - '

'Missing.'

'Presumed dead,' says Oliver.

'Missing persons turn up.'

'How often?'

'Often enough for you not to do anything rash,' says Jonty. 'Be patient. Wait.'

'Strong characters make things happen, Jonty. That's what the Earl always says. That's the principle I've been brought up with. The weak get swept along with the tide. For once in my life I want to make something happen. You said it yourself: some accept, some act.'

Jonty says nothing. An outsider, he thinks. He can't help visualising, superimposed over Oliver's face, an alabaster effigy of himself. He hears Izzie say, *Someone who's someone*. He remembers himself saying, *It's only a favour if it's what he wants.*

Oliver says, 'I need a favour, Jonty. I want to hire someone to... take care of things for me.'

'You mean a Contract?' says Jonty. 'With a capital C?'

'Yes,' says Oliver. 'A Contract.'

'I can get you a Contract,' says Jonty. 'But I can't do any more than that. I can't be involved. I can get you a Contract but after that you're on your own.'

33

Jonty is alone in the small, stone-flagged kitchen of the Dales hideaway. Yorkshire tea is stewing in the pot. Beyond the cottage window the slope of the valley is dotted with occasional sheep and crossed with dry stone walls. Wires dip and rise between telegraph poles.

The front door opens.

Izzie's voice says, 'It's me.'

Jonty looks up.

Izzie materialises in the kitchen doorway and pauses for effect. Instantly the world beyond the window feels more remote, the kitchen more immediate. She crosses the room, slumps into the chair opposite Jonty.

'Where have you been?' asks Jonty. 'I was worried.'

Izzie says, 'Here and there.'

'Not here.'

'There, then. Nowhere.'

'When I got back from Orvane you'd gone,' says Jonty. 'Vanished. I didn't know what had happened. Tea?'

Izzie nods.

Jonty pours.

She says, 'Nothing happened. Nothing does when you're dead.'

'Three days. I was worried.'

'Well I'm here now,' says Izzie. 'I was bored. No wonder they call this place Low Row. Low is the word.'

'But nobody saw you? Nobody recognised you?'

'No,' says Izzie. 'No one in this Godforsaken country knows who I am anyway.'

Jonty says, 'I doubt that. Anyway, while I was at Orvane something came up. A better solution. Eggs?'

'Better than what?'

'Better than you getting involved,' says Jonty.

'You're talking in riddles again. Yes please. Scrambled.'

Jonty goes to the fridge, takes out eggs, butter. He says, 'There's no need for that contract. I gave a copy to Ol. He wants to... hire someone. A contractor.'

'With a capital C?' asks Izzie.

'Yes. A Contractor.'

'You're kidding,' says Izzie. 'I didn't think he had it in him. I mean, I know he resents the Earl for treating you like the favoured son but I didn't think he would - '

'He what?'

'Resents the Earl,' says Izzie. 'But I didn't see this coming. I didn't think he would - '

'Hang on a minute,' says Jonty. He stops scrambling. 'You're saying Oliver thinks *I'm* the favoured one?'

'You are,' says Izzie. 'The Earl doesn't exactly go out of his way to hide it. Even I can see it. But I thought Oliver accepted it. He's always saying those were the cards he was dealt. But I didn't think he resented the Earl enough to do this.'

'Do what?'

'Help him along. Give him a nudge.' She nods at the bowl. 'Eggs.'

Jonty resumes scrambling.

He says, 'He's not helping the Earl along. The Contract is for himself. He thinks he's Romeo. He wants to join you in the hereafter.'

'Oh,' says Izzie. 'Cute.'

'I don't know about cute,' says Jonty. 'But there's no need for you to involve yourself.'

'I thought you said that would be a step too far? Helping Oliver.'

'Help is what he wanted,' says Jonty. 'He was asking for it.'

'You're sure this is the kind of help he was asking for?'

'It's his choice. He asked me for a Contract so I gave him a Contract.'

Jonty puts a pan on the Raeburn, pours in the eggs, looks for a wooden spoon.

Izzie says, 'You should have waited for the pan to get hot.'

'He was very specific,' says Jonty. 'So there's no need for you to sign one as well.'

'How do you know he'll go through with it?'

'I don't. But he sounded serious.'

'I've already signed.'

'Rescind,' says Jonty. 'Ask for a refund.'

'I can't.'

Jonty stirs. 'It's a distance sale. There's a statutory cooling off period. Consumer Contracts Regulations 2013.'

'You think Dean Stone is going to take any notice of that?'

'Who?'

'Dean Stone. My… contact. He's not going to take any notice of your stupid rules.'

'Regulations,' says Jonty. 'I suppose not.'

'It's... what's the word? Non-refundable. Uncancellable.'

'Irrevocable,' says Jonty.

'That too. So that's it. He's uncontactable.'

'Radio silence?' says Jonty. 'Under the radar?' He mimes a low-flying plane but the wooden spoon spoils the effect. 'Off the map?'

'When he's on a job he vanishes.'

'Hang on,' says Jonty. 'You mean you've done this before?'

'Not exactly,' says Izzie. 'What's that?'

'What?'

'That.' She points.

Jonty says, 'The *Yorkshire Post*.'

'I can see that, Jonty. It says "Yorkshire Post" at the top. Why is Oliver on the front page?'

'Don't know,' says Jonty. 'He's always popping up on the front for something or other.'

Izzie picks up the paper and shakes out the fold. Oliver's face smiles out from one of the teasers above the masthead. She reads, '*Inside: Eoferwic How Scarecrow Festival Souvenir Pullout*.'

'He must have stood in for the Earl,' says Jonty.

'What's a scarecrow festival when it's at home?'

'Skies and scarecrows,' says Jonty. 'East Yorkshire's famous for them. Skies and scarecrows, haystacks, hares and... something or other. Surely you have scarecrows in America?'

'Of course. I worked with one, remember.'

'Literally or metaphorically?'

'I was Dorothy?' Izzie's inflection is scathing. 'In the Wizard of Oz?'

'Oh,' says Jonty. 'It's not on your Wikipedia page.' He brings the eggs to the table. 'Here you go.'

'It was garbage,' admits Izzie.

'I'm sure you were brilliant.'

'I always am,' says Izzie. 'I was the only decent thing about it.' She takes a mouthful of eggs. 'Mmmm, good.' With her fork she points at the paper. 'You still haven't told me what a scarecrow festival is.'

Jonty shrugs. 'It's what it says on the tin.'

'What tin?'

'It's what you'd imagine,' says Jonty. 'Everyone makes a scarecrow. The whole town goes mad for it. There's a prize.'

Izzie opens the pullout. She reads, *'For the first time in over half a century the Earl of Eoferwic -'*

'He won't like that,' says Jonty. 'Not being able to judge the scarecrows. He must be on his last legs. Nothing gets between him and the scarecrows. I told you we should have waited.'

'And Oliver stood in for him?'

'Looks like it,' says Jonty.

Izzie says, 'He's carrying on as if nothing's happened.'

'Nothing has happened.'

'But he doesn't know that. He thinks I'm dead.'

'Missing,' says Jonty.

'Presumed dead. Yet he's going round judging scarecrow competitions as if everything's hunky dory. Scarecrow competitions!'

'Life goes on,' says Jonty.

'Well it shouldn't.'

212

'Steady,' says Jonty. 'You almost sound as if you care.'

'Is that the winner?' says Izzie. 'It looks like Oliver.'

Jonty says, 'Humpty Dumpty. All the king's horses and all the king's men.'

'They look like twins.'

Jonty looks at Izzie looking at Oliver.

Izzie says, 'What does Humpty Dumpty have to do with scaring crows?'

'The theme is n- '

'And what's that supposed to be? It looks like Anthony Perkins in Psycho.'

'Three blind mice,' says Jonty. 'The theme is nursery rhymes. You must remember Three Blind Mice?'

'No.'

'That's the farmer's wife with her carving knife. And those are the three blind mice.'

'They look like rats. They're going round in circles. Who's chasing who?'

'I suppose that depends on your perspective,' says Jonty. 'The mice ran after the farmer's wife. But it ended badly for the mice. She cut off their tails with the carving knife.'

'Nice.'

34

'I'm not dead, Jonty,' booms the Earl. 'Look at me. Do I look dead to you?'

'No,' says Jonty.

'Well then.'

'But according to Chichi Boo - '

'About as reliable as the weather forecast,' booms the Earl. 'I've told you before.'

'But her column. She said you were dead.'

'Well I'm not dead, am I? Don't believe everything you read in the press, Jonty. You should know that.'

'Yes,' says Jonty. 'I mean no.'

'I'm as right as rain.'

'Yes,' Jonty says again. 'As right as rain.'

'Hazel was always one for a bit of poetic licence,' says the Earl. 'Got that from her mother.' His laugh turns into a cough. 'But at least I'm in good company. They did the same thing to Churchill. What was it he said? "Rumours of my death have been greatly exaggerated." Marvellous.'

Jonty says, 'That was Mark Twain.'

'I thought it was Churchill?'

'Twain,' says Jonty. 'It was on the whiteboard at law school, the day we studied death and taxes.'

'Yes, well. Great sense of humour, Churchill. Even at death's door. He died a week after he cracked that joke. That rumour is probably what finished him off. Greatly exaggerated! Marvellous!' The Earl laughs until his laugh degenerates into a coughing fit.

Jonty waits.

The Earl recovers his breath. 'And my daughter-in-law. Two resurrections for the price of one. What do you make of that?'

Jonty looks away. He says, 'Lucky.'

'Bit of a coincidence, eh?' says the Earl. 'Bit odd.'

'Synchronicity,' says Jonty. 'Everyone's just glad you're both ok.'

'I'm sure they are,' booms the Earl. 'I'm sure they are. Bit of a coincidence that she came back to life the very day I died. Bit odd, that.'

'So long as you're both ok,' says Jonty.

'Keltbray said she was the top story on the *Yorkshire Post* website,' says the Earl. 'Whatever that means. Says she had amnesia. Washed up in Withernsea. Thought she was the lighthouse keeper's daughter. Talking broad Yorkshire, so he said.'

'I believe so,' says Jonty.

'Bit odd,' says the Earl.

Jonty says nothing.

'Bit of a coincidence.'

Jonty is content to let the conversation go round in circles. 'You're both ok, he says. That's all that matters.'

'Is it?' says the Earl.

'Better than both being dead,' says Jonty.

'We weren't both dead, though, were we Jonty? As soon as I died she came back to life. Bit of a coincidence, that, don't you think? Bit odd.'

Jonty says nothing.

'This amnesia,' says the Earl. 'Did she forget she was a Catholic?'

'What?' says Jonty.

'It's a simple question, Jonty. Did she forget she was a Catholic?'

'I... I don't know. I'm not involved. I don't know what goes on in her head.'

'Well you should know, Jonty. We've been through this before. It's what I pay you for, to know things. It rather brings us full circle, doesn't it?'

'Full circle?' says Jonty.

'Yes. Full circle. Back to where we were before her mysterious vanishment. Back to where we were before she got carried away.'

'Carried away?' says Jonty.

'Stop parroting, lad. Yes. Carried away. By the tide. We were about to execute a deed.'

The Earl takes the deed out his desk drawer.

'Oh,' says Jonty. 'Yes.'

'Well?'

'Is the deed really necessary?' says Jonty. 'After all everyone's been through? Are you sure you're well enough?'

'Well enough for what, Jonty? Well enough to write my name in a box? Of course I'm well enough, lad. Nothing like being dead to make you feel alive. I'll show her a thing or two about coming back to life. Never been better. Never - '

The Earl is interrupted by another coughing fit.

216

Jonty waits.

'Pass the pen,' says the Earl. He's still coughing.

'Are you sure about this?' says Jonty. The Mont Blanc stays in his pocket. 'Your son.'

'Jonty, is there something you know that I need to know?'

'No,' says Jonty.

'No known unknowns?'

'No,' says Jonty.

'No unknown unknowns?' More coughing.

'No,' says Jonty.

'How do you know what you don't know, lad?'

'I don't know,' says Jonty. 'I just know.'

'Well then,' says the Earl. He holds out his hand for the pen.

'We need a witness,' says Jonty. 'I can arrange someone for tomorrow.'

'Why can't you witness it?' asks the Earl.

'I'm not independent,' says Jonty.

'In what way?' says the Earl. 'You're not family.'

Not family. Jonty thinks quickly. Sometimes you have to play it by ear. This could be an insurance policy. 'OK,' he says. 'I'll bear witness.' He reaches into his jacket pocket and proffers the Mont Blanc between finger and thumb.

The Earl signs. 'Good.' He hands back the Mont Blanc. 'Nice pen. Where did you get that?'

'You gave it to me,' says Jonty. He returns the pen to his jacket pocket. 'You and Lady Mundayne. For my 21st.'

'Did we?' says the Earl. 'For your 21st? I don't remember that. Olivia must have chosen it. Always had good taste, Olivia. Always had an eye for the right thing.

217

Like me, eh Jonty?' The Earl laughs and coughs. 'She chose me!' He coughs again.

Jonty waits but the coughing doesn't subside. He moves towards the Earl.

The Earl holds up his hand. 'I'm fine,' he gasps, between coughs. 'I'm fine. Never been better. Right as rain.'

The coughing continues.

'Nothing wrong with me,' gasps the Earl. 'She chose me, Jonty. Olivia.'

The coughing subsides and stops.

Somewhere in the Hall a cuckoo clock sounds.

Better leave him to rest, thinks Jonty.

The Earl slumps forward. His dead hand slides the deed to Jonty's side of the desk. His head hits the blotter.

Shit, thinks Jonty. Shit.

He rounds the desk, drags the Earl out of his chair, stretches him out on the floor. He loosens the Earl's tie, rips open his shirt to start CPR. He hears the Earl's top three buttons hit the wall, then the floor. He tries to remember the timing. One-two-three-four, pause. One-two-three-four, pause. There's a sense of detachment. The sense that he's somewhere outside himself, watching himself, yet within himself, hearing himself count. Is he counting out loud? He hears himself shout for Keltbray, remembers it's Keltbray's day off. Higgins? Higgins will be in the garage. Too far. Mandy Howe? On her summer holiday. He watches himself continue the compressions with one hand, dial 999 with the other. Shit, he thinks. Shit. Come on. *Is the patient breathing?* No. Stop asking questions. Get a move on. *What's the patient's name?* His name? He's the bloody Earl of Eoferwic. *The Earl of Eoferwic?* Yes, the Earl of Eoferwic. *Isn't he dead? It was*

218

in the Yorkshire Post. It said - . 'He's not dead!' yells Jonty. 'Well, he wasn't then but he is now. Might be. Will be, if you don't get a move on. He's not breathing. Just get someone here.' *The ambulance is on its way.* 'On its way isn't good enough,' sobs Jonty. 'He was like a father to me. On its way isn't good enough. I need it here now.'

'It's on its way,' says the voice.

Jonty continues the compressions.

At last he hears shouts.

He calls, 'This way. In here.'

He's aware of boots and badges and uniforms and equipment. Monitors and gas canisters and latex gloves. The whine of a defibrillator.

He stands, backs away from the activity, opens the diamond-leaded window, sucks in air.

He notices the deed lying on the desk.

He picks up the deed and slips it into the inside pocket of his jacket.

35

'A glooming peace this morning with it brings,' intones the Reverend Martin. 'The sun, for sorrow, will not show his head.'

He raises both palms.

He's pleased with his choice of quotation. It seems apt. He smiles at his ingenuity. Then he remembers - sorrow. He imbues his smile with melancholy. He regrets his unruly eyebrows.

He senses the sightless gaze of the alabaster eyes, feels the hand of history on his shoulder.

The Earl is dead, he thinks, long live the Earl.

He looks at the coffin.

He looks at the new Earl and Countess, arm in arm in the front pew.

He looks at the dowager Countess beside them, leaning on Jonty's arm, pale behind her veil.

The new Countess looks as radiant as her predecessor does wan. An artful cross-fade. The dowager Countess weeps. The new Countess smiles. Her smile fills the nave. It ripples outwards until it encompasses the rest of St

Hilda's, then the churchyard, then the lawns and meadows and fountains of Orvane and then, via town and spinney and heathered moorland, reaches the original boundaries of the ancient Earldom.

The Rev looks at the coffin and the principal mourners and the pews beyond, most of them unoccupied, and reflects on how the Earl has outlived so many of his peers.

Ashes, he says. Dust.

Tea leaves, he thinks. Coffee spoons.

As he continues to intone, his gaze strays from the scattering of mourners to the empty niche on the north side of the transept. That niche has watched and waited patiently through the years, he thinks. Now its destiny is nigh. The niche is the same as always, yet somehow different now its occupant is imminent. Expectant of its new arrival. Fresh alabaster is due. Will it be a true likeness? thinks the Rev. Will it capture the essence of the Earl? His booming nature? He examines the other effigies. Are any of them true likenesses? Would any of us know? His gaze returns to the empty niche, then to the dowager Countess in the front pew. Will his alabaster hand reach out for hers? Or will his hands be folded over his chest, to be remodelled when the time comes? Will their voyage continue, unmapped, or does it end here, in alabaster?

Man that is born of woman, he says.

We commend unto Thy hands.

Afterwards, outside, among the leaning lichened slabs, there's a bright litter of birdcalls. The slow smoke of a late summer bonfire drifts through the trees.

Oliver says, 'Do you remember doing Larkin for GCSE?'

221

'GCSE?' says Jonty. 'Don't remember anything about that. I winged mine. The only thing exams - '

Oliver cuts him off. *'Aubade.'*

Jonty smiles. "Ow bad?'

'So you do remember.' Oliver's voice sounds wrong in his head. He feels artificial. The black suits and smoke make the scene feel unreal. He imagines Sal saying, Cut.

Jonty says, 'I remember the joke. I don't remember the poem.'

'No wonder,' says Oliver. 'I wrote your appraisal for you. You were too busy with Ann Hughes.'

'Who?'

'Never mind,' says Oliver. 'The point is, I couldn't make sense of it, then. Death seemed so remote. But I understand it now. The end being a whole day nearer; all that.' He glances across the gravestones to where Izzie is chatting with Olivia. 'Waking every day to the dread of dying.'

'Funerals do that to you,' says Jonty. 'Come on, let's go to the Eoferwic. Have a toast to the old man. My round.'

'It's not just the funeral, Jonty. It's more than that.' Oliver glances at the church clock. 'It's not just dawn marking another day nearer. It's every second of every minute. Every second is a second nearer. I can hear the clock ticking. Think about it. Not being here. Not being anywhere - and soon. That's the worst of it. Soon.'

'"Soon" could mean anything,' says Jonty. 'It's an undefined term. Come on.'

'Soon means soon, Jonty. That damned Contract. I signed it.'

'Ah,' says Jonty. 'The Contract. So you went through with it?'

'Of course I went through with it,' says Oliver. 'I told you, for once in my life I wanted to steer my own course. What did you think I was going to do with it? Roll it up and smoke it? Appraise it for the class? Well done Mundayne. A+. Your prize is to be first in line for a date with death.'

'I thought it would ease the pressure,' says Jonty. 'Knowing there was a way out. I thought it would make it bearable. I didn't think you'd actually sign it.'

'I wanted to be with Izzie.'

Jonty is silent.

'I still do. Despite...' Oliver looks across the churchyard at Izzie. 'I thought her eyes had looked their last,' he says. 'I thought our arms had shared their last embrace. So I made a bargain with engrossing death. I signed it with that damned pen you gave us.'

'That pen is designed by Pininfarina,' says Jonty. 'The people who fit out Ferraris. It's the Rolls Royce of pens.'

'But now she's here, in this world,' continues Oliver. 'And I want to be here with her. The bargain is dateless, Jonty. A dateless bargain with engrossing death. It could happen at any moment. He could be on his way. Or she. Death could be landing at Yeadon as we speak.'

'Or Humberside,' says Jonty. 'Anna flew from Humberside. She said there were good onward connections.'

'Anna had a bike.'

'Robin Hood, then,' says Jonty. 'That would be appropriate. For an outlaw.'

Oliver says, 'No assassin worth their salt is going to travel via Doncaster Airport.'

'I suppose not.'

'What can I do, Jonty? I'm worried. I'm a worried man with a worried mind. I'm standing on the gallows with my head in the noose. How do I cancel?'

'You can't,' says Jonty. 'It's irrevocable.'

'What does that mean?'

'It means it can't be revoked.'

'Obviously.'

'Well then.'

'I mean what does it *mean*,' says Oliver. 'For me. It's my money. The customer is always right.'

'Let me have a think,' says Jonty.

'There's no time to think,' says Oliver. He glances again at the church clock. 'What about changing the name in the box? Changing the target? What about a boar? We've got plenty of boar. Or what about just paying them to do nothing?'

Jonty says, 'They're uncontactable.'

The clock strikes one.

'Things will look better over a Black Sheep,' says Jonty. 'Come on.'

They sit at the end of the bar.

'So?' asks Oliver.

'Well,' says Jonty. 'You could play dead. Lie low for a couple of weeks. I know a little place in the Dales. If you're dead they can't kill you.'

'You mean, set something up? Like Lucky Lucan?'

'Why not?' says Jonty. 'No target, no hit.'

'What happens when I come back to life?'

'Ah,' says Jonty. 'Yes. Well. We can cross that bridge when we come to it.'

'Can we? Won't we just be back here again? Full circle? There must be another way out. I can't play dead for the rest of my life.'

36

'Things have changed.'

'What things?'

'All things,' says Izzie. 'Everything.'

Jonty swigs the last of his tea. He gives her a look. 'Changed how?'

'Changed back. To how they were before.'

'Before what?'

'Before they changed.'

'So things are the same?'

'Yes. No. This time round it's different. Me and Oliver, we… I… It has to stop, Jonty.'

'What has to stop?'

'This.' She indicates Jonty's kitchen. 'Us.'

'Oh.'

'And Oliver worrying about the Contract,' says Izzie. 'That has to stop, too. We need a way out.'

'We?'

'Me and Oliver. We - I - I'm asking for your help, Jonty. As a friend.'

'Oh, I… As a friend. Right-oh.' Jonty pulls a legal pad across the kitchen table. He uncaps the Mont Blanc. 'If you could get hold of your mate you could ask him to change the name in the box.' On the yellow pad he writes "Change name in box". He adds a question mark.

'I never said he's my mate. I said he's someone I know.'

'But he owes you a favour.' Jonty writes "FAVOUR". He underlines it twice. 'There must be a way of getting hold of him.'

'We've been through this,' says Izzie. 'We're going round in circles.'

Jonty writes "CIRCLES". He crosses out "CIRCLES". He says, 'Well…'

Izzie says, 'There's something else. There might be two Contracts.'

'There were always two Contracts. Yours is irrelevant. Your target died, remember.'

'There might be a complication,' says Izzie. 'Oliver is the Earl of Eoferwic, right?'

'Yes. The Earl is dead, long live the Earl. The title is perpetual. When the Earl died Oliver became the Earl. What does that have to do with anything?'

'I wrote "Earl of Eoferwic" in the box.'

'Oh.' On the pad Jonty draws a hangman.

He says, 'Well, even Oliver can't be killed twice.'

'So I'm right? There are two Contracts?'

Jonty adds a crosspiece to the gallows. 'Depends exactly what you wrote in the box.'

'I told you, I wrote "Earl of Eoferwic".'

'Just that?' says Jonty. 'Not "The 12th Earl of Eoferwic"? Not "Marmaduke Mundayne, Earl of Eoferwic"?'

'Like I said, I put "Earl of Eoferwic". That's what he is, isn't it? Was. That's who was standing in my way. Holding things up. Refusing to budge. I blame the Earl.'

'Oliver is the Earl.'

'He wasn't when I signed the Contract.'

'If you wrote Earl of Eoferwic in the box the Contract is for the Earl of Eoferwic,' says Jonty. 'Oliver is the Earl of Eoferwic.'

'He can't know there are two Contracts, Jonty. He's worried enough about one. He keeps saying he's waiting on the last train. Expecting all hell to break loose. There must be a way out.'

'Let's look at this in the round,' says Jonty. 'Let's consider all the facts. Two Contracts.' He draws a vertical line down the centre of the legal pad. 'Oliver took out a Contract in his own name.' Jonty writes "Viscount Mundayne" at the top of the first column. 'And you took out a contract in the name of the Earl of Eoferwic.' He writes "Earl of Eoferwic" at the top of the second column. He looks at the two columns. 'There,' he says. 'Now we know where we stand. The issues are clear.'

'Can't we explain?' asks Izzie.

'Explain what?'

'That the Viscount isn't the Viscount and the Earl isn't the Earl.'

'And you're not you and I'm not me?' says Jonty. 'No. Oliver is still Viscount. And now he's Earl as well. He's both. And if you wrote "Earl of Eoferwic" in the box that makes it an express term of the contract.'

'What does that mean?'

'It means you've paid someone to kill the Earl of Eoferwic.'

'Oh my God. When you put it like that… What about the cooling down period? You said there's a cooling down period.'

'Cooling off period,' says Jonty. 'The cooling off period is fourteen days. Fourteen days expired yesterday.' He picks up his empty mug and takes a virtual swig of non-existent tea. 'Anyway, you said Dave wouldn't take any notice of the Consumer Contract Regulations 2013.'

'Dean.'

'And you said he's uncontactable.'

'Someone must be able to contact him.'

'Who?' says Jonty. 'He's your friend.'

'I never said he's my friend. I said he's someone I know.'

'Whatever.'

Izzie says, 'You sound like me.' She laughs. She reaches for Jonty's hand.

Jonty's hand reaches for his empty mug. 'I thought things had changed?'

'Oh,' says Izzie. 'Yes.' She retracts her hand.

Jonty nods. He lifts the mug. 'Tea?'

'Is that the British answer to everything?'

'It helps.' Jonty crosses the kitchen to make tea.

'Someone must be checking messages,' says Izzie. 'In case they get another booking.'

Jonty fills the kettle. 'We can't just leave a message. People ignore messages.' He puts the kettle on the hob. 'Hang on a minute. That's it.'

'That's it?'

'The answer,' says Jonty. 'You just said "in case they get another booking". That's it. We take out another Contract.'

He returns to the table, writes "Another Contract."

228

'How is another Contract going to help? Two Contracts is worse than one, so how would three Contracts be better than two? When you're in a hole, stop digging. That's what Anna always says.'

'With respect,' says Jonty, 'Anna is not trained in the law of England and Wales. This is my jurisdiction. Nothing will come of nothing. My advice is to keep digging.'

Izzie sighs. 'How will another Contract solve anything?'

'First Law of Escalation,' says Jonty. 'Escalate.'

'Escalate?'

'Alright, proliferate. It's like lies. Lies beget lies. They keep on growing. Like flies round shit. If we can't call off the dogs we'll call in more dogs.'

'More dogs?'

'Stop repeating everything I say.'

'You're not making sense.'

Jonty says, 'It's simple. We take the BOGOF.' He writes "BOGOF" on the legal pad. 'We hire another one to bump off the first two. If you've got the original booking reference it won't cost a penny extra.'

Izzie gives him a look.

'Izzie, you have got the original booking reference? First Law of Online Shopping. Always keep the - '

'I'll find it,' says Izzie. 'But what if the other two get here first?'

'We stipulate that time is of the essence. If time is of the essence the third one has to do his job before the other two can do any damage. Basic contract law.'

'You're sure that'll work?'

'Trust me,' says Jonty. 'I'm a lawyer.'

37

Robin Hood Airport is shrouded in mist.

A man in a long black coat stifles a yawn.

Breakfast, he thinks.

He stops, scans the amber overhead signage for a knife and fork, nods, rides the escalator to the mezzanine food zone.

He finds a table looking out over where the runways should be. Beyond the windows the mist is fathomless. Occasionally there's a sense of sound and speed - a swirling disturbance in the greyish-white. Planes are still arriving and departing.

A waitress arrives.

The man in the long black coat asks, 'Where are we?'

'Here,' says the waitress. She gestures with her pad at the blank window.

The man in the long black coat looks at her. He senses a plane taking off. He thinks, On a clear day its angle of ascent would be reflected in her eyes.

She says, 'Doncaster-Sheffield.'

'Which?'

'Both,' she says. 'Neither.'

He points at the full English.

She draws a hieroglyph on her pad. She says, 'Between.'

He nods.

She departs.

The man in the long black coat removes his military-issue boots, flexes his toes, puts his boots back on.

Another waitress appears, with coffee. As she slides it across the table there's another perturbation in the static beyond the window.

The man in the long black coat raises his coffee to his lips, pauses before it makes contact, puts it back on the saucer. Too hot.

He turns his back to the window and looks down through the glass perimeter of the mezzanine into the well of the concourse below. He sees a man in a long black coat stifle a yawn, scan the amber overhead signage, nod, ride the escalator to the food zone.

At the top of the escalator the second man stumbles. His wheelie-bag is trapped between the relentless rise of the steel steps and the continuous descent of the rubber handrail. He wrenches the wheelie-bag free, drags it with him. He finds a table, parks the wheelie-bag, stares at the blank white wall of window. A waitress appears, takes his order, returns with coffee, slides it across the table.

The first man looks at the second. The second man looks at nothing.

The second man slurps his coffee, scalding his mouth.

Beyond the glass perimeter of the mezzanine, unseen by either of the men in long black coats, a man in a long

231

black coat strides across the concourse and onto the forecourt where he raises his arm for a cab.

The waitress arrives with two full English breakfasts. She slides one across one table, the other across the other. Beyond the window the mist swirls.

The first man forks an over-fried mushroom and presses it into his egg until the yolk bursts. He watches the slow flow of golden-yellow. He thinks, Why am I here?

The second man lifts a forkful of black pudding to his mouth and makes a face. He puts down his fork, still loaded, and pushes away his plate. He scans the signage and heads off towards the railway platforms.

Minutes later the second man returns for his wheelie-bag. He's surprised to see the wheelie-bag and his unfinished breakfast still there, where he'd left them.

He sits, resumes eating.

The first man stands, scans the overhead signage and heads to the car hire zone.

He drives away, his eyes on the road, his hands upon the wheel, heading for the M18.

Later, swerving east, away from the rich industrial shadows of Ferrybridge and Drax, the M18 becomes the M62, running now between thin and thistled fields, then the M62 becomes the A63, running parallel to the railway line.

In the wing mirror of the hire car the first man sees a train gaining on him. Not train, he thinks: electric multiple unit. EMU. It looks closer than it should, as if it's on the hard shoulder of the dual carriageway instead of the railway tracks. It slides from wing mirror to passenger window to quarterlight as it draws alongside and pulls ahead, then from quarterlight to passenger window to wing mirror as it falls back alongside and drops behind.

We will shortly be arriving at Brough.

On the EMU, the second man stares out of the carriage window. He sees a hire car swerve into the middle lane to avoid the back of an articulated truck.

His eyes shift focus and he's staring at himself in the window. He sees nothing beyond. Only his reflection, with its ghost, trapped between the panes of the double-glazed panel.

The train jerks to a halt.

His wheelie-bag slides off the luggage rack.

The third man has already checked into the Eoferwic Arms and is beginning his recce. He circles St Hilda's. An alibi, should he need one. *I came to see the famous spire.* Not spire, he thinks. Spires aren't squat and square. I came to see the ancient Norman tower. He goes inside, makes notes. *Serpents, ammonites,* he reads. *Fossils*, he writes. He crosses the road, rounds the bend, makes a mental note of the roadside stream, the roughstone bridge. He glances up at the sculpted wild boar, one on each gatehouse roof. He glances down the Avenue, the twin lines of lime trees framing Orvane like a doll's house.

Later, running from tree to tree under cover of darkness, he's disoriented by their repeated sameness silhouetted against the night sky, black on black. First he has the impression the Hall is moving towards him on rails, expanding as it approaches, looming ever larger. Then the impression changes and he's continuously running into the orbit of the same tree, moving but going nowhere.

Ahead of him, two dark figures are doing the same, one on each side of the Avenue, each oblivious to the

233

other and both oblivious to the third man behind them: three dark shapes on a synchronised stationary voyage.

Beneath his breath the third man murmurs, 'See how they run.'

38

'What's that?'

'Nothing.'

'It's not nothing,' says Oliver.

'Something, then. A raccoon.'

'We don't have raccoons, Izzie. It's the East Riding.'

'A squirrel, then.'

'Shh, listen.'

Izzie says, 'It's nothing.'

'It's something,' says Oliver. 'It's him. Come on.'

'Him?'

'The Contractor.'

'I thought you said Jonty had sorted that?'

'Obviously not,' says Oliver. 'He probably didn't have time. He said he had late night negotiations in Goole. Come on.' He takes Izzie's hand, pulls her out of bed.

'What are you doing? Where are we going?'

'Shh. I'll tell you when we get there. Here, put your slippers on.' He passes Izzie her slippers. 'And this.' He reaches under the bed, pulls out two Barbours and passes one to Izzie. He says, 'There are supplies in the poachers' pockets. Nuts and raisins.'

They put on their Barbours and tiptoe to the door.

Slowly Oliver turns the knob, opens the door, scans the hallway.

'Come on.' He grabs Izzie's hand.

Seventy miles away, in Leeds, Oliver and Izzie drift silently from screen to screen across a series of fuzzy monitors in an empty operations room.

Behind them a dark shadow ghosts through the same frames.

The security operative is in what passes for a kitchen, waiting for the kettle to boil. He yawns.

In the empty operations room, on one of the monitors, Oliver leads Izzie through the door to the back stairs.

They descend out of sight of the camera.

The shadow follows, closes the door quietly behind him.

The security operative returns to his high-backed chair, tea in hand, and scans the screens. All is as it was. Nothing is occurring.

He swivels his chair away from the monochrome monitors, returns his attention to Babestation, in colour.

He sips his tea.

On the monitor behind him Oliver and Izzie emerge from the stairwell into the wine cellar.

The shadow waits.

'I took a leaf out of the American book,' whispers Oliver. 'I got Abram to set up a panic room. Over here, look. Where you filmed Juliet's... erm... final scene. There's a memory-foam mattress and a composting toilet. We can survive for weeks.'

236

'I can't be underground for weeks on end! I've got a movie to promote.'

'Think of Orpheus and Eurydice,' says Oliver. 'Dante and Beatrice. Remember Battlefield? This is our katabasis. It's a sign of true love.'

'Kata-what?'

'Journey into the underworld,' says Oliver. 'When we emerge we'll be reborn.'

He opens the door of the panic room. 'Come on, we'll be safe in here.'

From within a voice says, 'Are you Mundayne?'

'Who's that?' Oliver steps back, shielding Izzie.

A gun appears in the doorway. An arm follows. A man in a long black coat steps out of the panic room.

Oliver backs away, keeping Izzie behind him.

'Never mind who I am,' says the man in the long black coat. 'Are you Mundayne?'

'Yes,' says Oliver.

'Viscount Mundayne?'

'Yes,' says Oliver.

The man in the long black coat says, 'Special delivery.' He cocks the gun. 'Have a nice day.'

A voice says, 'Wait.'

Jonty steps out from behind one of the pillars supporting the vaulted wine cellar. He says, 'I'm Viscount Mundayne.'

The gun moves from Oliver to Jonty and back again.

Izzie gasps. 'What are you - ?'

Jonty stops her with a shake of his head.

The gunman says, 'Don't mess with me. Which one of you is Viscount Mundayne?'

'Me,' says Jonty. The gun moves to Jonty, the eyes stay on Oliver.

'I am,' says Oliver. The gun moves to Oliver, the eyes move to Jonty.

The gunman says, 'One of you is lying.'

'Obviously,' says Jonty. 'Unless we're both lying. Or unless there are two Viscount Mundaynes. Perhaps there are no Viscount Mundaynes at all.'

Oliver says, 'Jonty, what are you - '

'Is that right?' continues Jonty. 'Viscount Mundaynes? Or should that be "Viscounts Mundayne"? He raises his hands to draw the inverted commas in the air.

The gun swings towards him.

He lowers his hands.

'One of us can only lie,' says Jonty. 'The other can only tell the truth.'

The eyes stay on Jonty, the gun returns to Oliver. 'Which one lies?'

Jonty says, 'Viscount Mundayne.'

'Right,' says the gunman. 'That's it.'

A voice says, 'Wait.'

Another gun appears from behind another pillar. Another arm follows. Another long black coat steps forward. 'Which one of you is the Earl of Yoffer-wyke?'

'Everwick,' says Oliver. 'It's pronounced "Everwick".'

One gun points at Oliver, then at Jonty. The other points at Jonty, then at Oliver.

'Which one of you is the Earl?'

Jonty says, 'There is no Earl.' He reaches for the deed in the inside pocket of his jacket. Both guns swing towards him. He lowers his hand.

The second gunman cocks his gun.

A voice says, 'Wait.'

238

A man in a long black coat emerges from the stairwell, a gun in each hand, one trained on each of the other long black coats.

Everybody turns.

One of the gunmen says, 'Wait, what?'

The other says, 'Mr Stone?'

'Well now,' says Stone. 'We appear to have ourselves a situation.'

39

'Well now,' says Stone. 'What's this?'

'A deed.'

'I can see it's a deed, Bagshawe. It says "Deed" at the top.'

Jonty says, 'It's Fullerton-Bagshawe. With a hyphen.'

'Names mean nothing' says Stone.

Jonty says, 'A rose - '

'Quiet!'

Stone keeps his guns trained on the men in the long black coats.

The men in the long black coats keep their guns trained on Jonty and Oliver.

Stone says, 'What do I want with a deed?'

'It's not an ordinary deed,' says Jonty. 'It's unusual.'

'What's unusual about it?'

'It renders everything null and void.'

'How so?'

'Moments before he died,' says Jonty, 'the late Earl cut off his heir.'

'Don't mess with me, Bagshawe. I'm not in the mood. I've had a long flight.'

Jonty says, 'He executed - '

'Have you any idea what it's like being a hitman, Bagshawe? People think it's glamorous. They think it's all long black coats and military-issue boots and sleek steel sidearms. But it's not. It's not, let me tell you. It's redeye flights and interminable taxi rides and hard beds in unpronounceable hotels. It plays havoc with your telomeres.'

Jonty says nothing.

'So don't tell me a rich man's dying wish was a visit to the barbershop.'

'No,' says Jonty.

'What, then?'

'Not hair,' says Jonty. 'Heir. The Earl decided to disinherit. His last act was to execute this deed.' He holds up the deed. 'So there is no Earl. The Twelfth Earl was the end of the line.'

Oliver stares at Jonty. 'What? Jonty, that's exc - '

'Not now,' says Jonty.

Izzie steps out from behind Oliver. 'What? Jonty, don't tell me - '

'Not now,' says Jonty.

'Perdy!' says Stone. 'Fancy meeting you here. Do you come here often?'

'That's Lady Markham to you.'

'Gone up in the world, Perdy?' says Stone. 'Found yourself another new identity?'

'Not now,' says Izzie.

'If you say so, Sis.' Stone turns to Jonty. 'What does that' - he nods at the deed - 'have to do with this?' He indicates the circle of guns.

241

'Well,' says Jonty. 'It's complicated.'

'Try me.'

'His contract' - Jonty points the deed at the second man - 'is for Viscount Mundayne. And his contract' - he points the deed at the first - 'is for the Earl of Eoferwic. And yours' - he doesn't point - 'is for the, er… pursuers of Viscount Mundayne and the Earl of Eoferwic. But thanks to this deed' - he holds up the deed - 'Viscount Mundayne and the Earl of Eoferwic no longer exist. So everything is null and void. Everyone can go back to bed.'

Oliver says, 'Jonty, is there something we need to disc- '

'Everything's in hand,' says Jonty. 'Trust me.'

'Null and void?' says Stone. 'Null and void! I don't think so. These Contracts are irrevocable.'

'But there are no targets,' says Jonty. 'So there can be no specific performance. And in any event yours is a Prime Contract.'

'So?'

'So time is of the essence.'

'What in hell does that mean?'

'It means your contract needs to be performed first,' says Jonty. 'So either the Contracts are null and void or you need to shoot your henchmen before they shoot us.'

Stone waves his gun at the first man.

'Flower,' he says. 'Call Anna. Ask her what the Contract says about targets. Ask her what it says about me shooting you and... what's his name?'

The second man says, 'The name's Duff. Milton Duff.' From the panic room comes the sound of a wheelie-bag falling over.

Flower looks at his watch. He says, 'It's three in the morning. Anna will be asleep.'

242

'She's in LA,' says Stone. 'She's eight hours behind.'

'Are you sure?' says Jonty. 'We're on British Summer Time, remember.'

Duff says, 'You call this summer?'

'Summer is always like this,' says Jonty.

'Actually,' he says, 'it's not always like this. My first summer at Orvane was the exception that proves the rule. That was a proper summer. Ol, do you remember that summer? It went on till autumn.'

Flower says, 'O season of mists and mellow fruitfulness.'

'There was even a hosepipe ban.'

'Enough already!' says Stone. 'Enough with the time difference, enough with the hosepipe bans, enough with the mists and mellow fruitfulness. Flower, call Anna.'

Flower's gun is still on Oliver. With his free hand he extricates his phone from his pocket. Beneath his breath he mutters, 'Close bosom-friend of the maturing sun.'

Stone says, 'What did you say?'

'Nothing,' says Flower.

Jonty says, 'If you're talking to Anna, tell her the Earl left her his bike collection.'

Flower tries to key in a code one-handed, with his thumb. He drops the phone.

Jonty says, 'He left everything else to the National Trust.'

With his gun still on Oliver, Flower bends, picks up the phone, thumbs in the code, stares at the screen. He says, 'No signal.'

Stone says, 'We need a new deal.'

'Yes,' says Izzie. 'I think we do.'

'Bagshawe, you're an attorney.'

'Solicitor,' says Jonty. 'Second oldest profession. And it's *Fullerton*-Bagshawe. With a hyphen. Shall I pop upstairs and get my practising certificate?' He mimes lifting a picture frame off a wall.

'No. No certificates.'

'I can make us all a nice cup of tea while I'm at it,' says Jonty. 'Do you all take milk?' He mimes pouring milk. 'I can be mother.'

'No!' says Stone.

'No milk?' Jonty mimes a jug hovering over a cup.

'No tea,' says Stone. 'No certificates. No one leaves this room. And enough with the stupid hand gestures.'

Izzie says, 'Dean. This is really very simple. No one wants what's in those Contracts. Not even you.'

She takes Oliver's hand.

'My husband and I want to remarry. You get your money either way. So for once in your life don't stand in my way.'

'You're in the wrong town, Sis. You should be in Hollywood.'

'Don't stand in my way, Dean. Let me have what I want.'

'Which is?'

'To stop going round in circles. For history to stop repeating itself.' She looks into Oliver's eyes. 'We want to renew our vows.'

Oliver nods.

Stone says, 'Shall we all pause for a moment to consider the intellectual poverty of that proposition? You want to stop history repeating itself by redoing something you've already done?'

'You pompous ass. Some things never change. You always were a pompous ass, Dean, and you always will be a pompous ass. Big brother doesn't always know best. I mean it. We want to renew our vows. We want to live the dream. Like Romeo and Juliet.'

'Are you sure?' says Oliver. 'That didn't end well. You died, remember? Right here, in this vault.'

'Whatever,' says Izzie. 'Dandy and Beatrice, then. You said this is our kata-what's-it. You said we'll be reborn. We can start over.'

'Dante and Beatrice didn't get together till they were dead,' says Oliver. 'Why don't we just try being ourselves? You never know what might happen.'

Ian Caro was born in Castleford and lives on the Isle of Wight. He has worked as a stage manager, a lighting designer, a ghost writer and a lawyer, and currently provides pre-publication legal advice to a number of national and regional news publishers.

SPURN is his second novel.